TROUBLE BREWING

A PARKER LEE MYSTERY

M.P. BLACK

For the many storytellers—living and dead—who taught me. Thank you.

1

"Oh, no," Ray groaned.

"What?" I asked.

"Break-in."

He pointed to the front door of the Breeze. Someone had crowbarred the lock, shattering the surrounding wood.

Ray stepped away from the door and cursed.

"They messed with the camera, too."

I looked up. A security camera perched on a brick ledge near the big sign that said, "Lake Breeze Brewery & Restaurant." But the burglar had covered the lens with what looked like a giant wad of gum.

"I'll call Mom," I said, digging my phone out of my pocket.

"Thanks," Ray said. "I'll call Roxie."

Roxie, Ray's wife, was his business partner. She managed the Breeze, handling finances and marketing, while my brother Ray took care of day-to-day operations at the bar and brewery. He was both co-owner and brewmaster.

I'd joined him this morning to get ideas for an article I'd

write for *The Allington Gazette* on the Breeze. It was Roxie's idea. Part of a marketing campaign they were running, which included posters throughout town. *The Gazette*, being a local paper, wasn't above giving local businesses a little extra love. Plus, it was my family. I wasn't above giving my family a little extra love.

But now this might turn into a front-page story about burglary instead.

Mom answered her cell phone. "Hey, Park."

In the background, I could hear voices, someone typing, and another phone ringing—the sounds of the Allington Police Department.

I told her about what happened and she promised to get down to the docks as quick as possible.

Ray said, "Let's go take a look at the damage."

"They can't have gotten away with much," I said, hoping to say something encouraging. "They'd need a boat to transport anything valuable. And that would be pretty conspicuous."

I gestured at the lake behind us. The Breeze occupied a brick building that used to be a warehouse for the lake trade back when Allington's biggest business was lumber. It was the town's favorite restaurant and bar. The place was often packed with tourists, every table under the awnings on the docks occupied—and locals gathered for dates and sports games and even the occasional wedding reception.

But this early on a Wednesday morning, the docks were abandoned. Out on the lake, a fisherman sat in his rowboat, patiently waiting for a catch. A bird dove into the water near Gull Island and then bobbed up again. The water shimmered. The sky was cloudless and blue. As if scrubbed clean after last night's rain.

"Guess we'll find out," Ray said, pulling open the door.

Inside, the bar and restaurant smelled of hardwood, beer, and barbecue. A good smell. As I followed Ray, I surveyed the space: the long wooden bar counter, the tables with the chairs stacked on top, and the booths. No sign of damage.

Ray went behind the bar and checked the liquor bottles.

"The burglar's been back here," he said. "Took a couple of bottles of bourbon."

"Expensive stuff?"

Ray shook his head. "I don't carry the cheapest brands, but this wasn't the premium stuff."

"What about the cash register?"

"It's open. Doesn't matter, though. It's empty." He shut the register with a bang. "We empty it every night and put the cash in our safe. The burglar must've been pretty disappointed."

"So the person just stole some bourbon and then bolted," I said. "That's not too bad."

"No, not too bad. We just have to fix the front door. But I'd better check the brewery."

I followed him to the back of the bar. A big sign on the door said, "DANGER: Staff Only." Ray pushed open the door. In the brewery, wooden floorboards gave way to white tile. A row of shiny metal tanks crowded the space. Pipes leading to each tank. More pipes criss-crossing the ceiling. On the side of each tank was a sign that said, "Danger: HOT."

At the far end, the ceiling opened, and the building expanded upward, leaving space for a row of massive fermentation tanks. They reminded me of silos.

Everything was tidy and clean.

"Looks fine," I said.

Ray rubbed the back of his neck, looking uncertain. "I

sure hope so. We've been brewing new batches and preparing for the weekend. We can hardly keep up with demand. Yesterday, we got everything ready for fermentation."

He wandered from tank to tank, checking gauges and looking behind the big metal kettles.

"This looks good," he said.

He moved down the brewery toward the back, and I followed him into the high-ceilinged area with the fermentation tanks. Ray stopped. A dead stop.

"Something's not right."

"What?"

I looked around. I saw nothing out of the ordinary. Everything was obsessively clean. Just those massive silo-like metal tanks.

Ray climbed a ladder to a narrow walkway along the tanks. I stayed below.

"No," he groaned, as he checked a set of gauges. "No, no, no..."

"What?"

He turned toward me. A look of despair on his face.

"The burglar must've messed with the thermostats." He turned back around, moving down the walkway to the next tank. He cursed. "This one, too. And this one, too."

Ray ran down the metal stairs and raced to a spigot at the bottom of one of the tanks. He grabbed a cup from a rack nearby and opened the spigot. Murky liquid spilled into the cup. He took a sip and grimaced.

"This can't be happening..."

He ran to the next vat and opened the spigot and tasted the beer there, too. And grimaced again.

"I don't get it," I said. "What happens if you tamper with the thermostats?"

Ray faced me. He leaned against the vat, as if to steady himself.

"It means trouble, Parker. The temperature's too high, which causes the yeast to produce more esters and phenols. The taste is way off. Plus, there's a risk of bacterial contamination."

"Which means...?"

"Which means we've got to start over. We've got to empty all the vats, throwing everything out." He ran a hand through his hair and let out a long breath. "This is a big blow to the business."

2

After Mom and Deputy Douglas arrived, I decided to leave Ray to cope with the disaster. He didn't need my support, anyway. Roxie was on her way —although first she needed to drop off Wimsey, their Dalmatian, at a neighbor's house.

I stepped outside to a gloriously sunny day. Several sailboats cut across Lake Allington and high above me, the single-propeller plane from Allington Tours made a circuit.

My stomach felt off-kilter. Like I was a little seasick. How could something so awful happen on such a beautiful day?

The Breeze would be fine. It would have to be. Roxie would sweep in and get everyone working twice as hard so they could catch up. And she'd make sure Ray was fine, too.

Of course she would.

Even so, I worried. Part of me could never forget the dark periods my brother had gone through when he was younger. I'd been a kid then, but I could still remember the weeks and weeks of Ray not talking to anyone. The closed door. The dark, brooding music vibrating through the wall.

Down at the end of the docks, my other brother, Scottie,

was busy unrolling the awning over his ice cream shop. I was tempted to head over and say hello—mostly to tell him about the break-in—but the family grapevine would inform him soon enough.

Besides, I was late for work at *The Gazette*, and I had a deadline for another story today. If I could knock that one out quickly, I could get the burglary story started, too. It was important news. I only hoped that it wouldn't do further damage to Ray and Roxie's business.

I headed down the docks, away from the direction of Scottie's Ice Cream Shop. My sneakers padded on the boards. Beneath them, the water sloshed against the pilings. I could see the water moving down there in the gloom and I could see—

I stopped. What was that?

A card. I crouched down and picked it up.

It was about the size of a credit card. Heavy paper stock. Glossy. Bright colors, which was why it caught my eye. But it was frayed at the edges, and so badly rubbed and water-logged that its print had worn out. Still, the image on the front was obviously an illustration of Jesus.

I straightened up, and flipping it over, saw a text printed on the back. Most of it had been ruined by the rain. It was difficult to read. "God grant me"—the next part was illegible —"to accept the"—illegible again—"know the difference."

Must be a prayer of some sort.

Even I could work that out.

Down in the bottom right-hand corner, which was torn and frayed, it said, "Concord." Though that might only be half of the text, since the other half was too frayed to read. Concord was a place, of course. Concord, New Hampshire. Concord, Massachusetts. Wasn't there a Concord in California, too?

As I was considering the card, I glanced up and noticed that one of the old souvenir shops had closed. Now, signs announced a new business opening soon. A man in blue overalls on a ladder was hanging a sign that said, "Wine Bar."

A new wine bar? I'd have to ask around about that.

Then this popped into my mind: Concord grapes.

I looked down at the card I'd found again. Did the Jesus card have something to do with the wine bar? I shook my head at myself. Concord grapes were used for juice, not wine. Not usually, anyway. Maybe a tourist dropped it. Probably just trash. But even small mysteries could keep me up at night—like a crossword puzzle left undone.

So I stuffed it into my pocket.

3

At the end of the docks, I turned up Main Street. Passing the municipal parking lot, I spotted Dani D'Angelo, and my heart sank.

I liked Dani. Brown buzzcut. Big brown eyes. Lots of piercings in her ears and nose, and a big yin-yang tattoo on her left shoulder. She had the kind of open, friendly face that made her instantly likable. At least to me.

But right now, I didn't want to talk to her. She was an assistant brewer and bartender at the Breeze. And I didn't want to be the bearer of bad news.

As I hurried past the parking lot, she was halfway out of her car, a beat-up red Toyota Camry that must've changed hands a dozen times. She locked the car, actually turning a key in a lock (no bleep-bleep for this old clunker), and then looked up. Her eyes zeroing right in on me.

"Parker—hey!"

I froze.

There was a spring to her step. An eagerness as she headed toward me.

"You're sprightly this morning," I mumbled. "Aren't you, like, many hours early for work?"

She laughed. "Yeah, and I'm totally suffering from sleep deprivation. I was at the brewery late last night. Then got home and could hardly sleep. Not with the latest batch we've worked on being ready for testing. I wanted to get to the Breeze early so I could see how the beer's doing."

I rubbed the back of my neck. I couldn't pretend nothing had happened. I was about to write about it in *The Gazette*, for crying out loud. I shouldn't be running away from Dani. A journalist's job was to talk to people.

So talk I would.

I let out a long sigh. Nothing like delivering bad news to someone so happy.

"Listen, Dani," I said. "Something's happened..."

As I told her, she put a hand in front of her mouth. Her eyes went wide.

"No," she said. "That can't be true. Why would someone do that? I mean, I get it if someone steals booze from the bar. But why would they tamper with our fermentation? Why would anyone—?" She stopped. Looked off into the distance, frowning. "If I find out who did this..." Then shook her head and sighed. "Why would someone do such a thing?"

"Yeah, I honestly don't know, either," I said. "My mom's there now with Deputy Douglas, and I'm sure they'll investigate."

What I didn't mention was that I knew how many burglaries got solved in Allington. Not a lot. Most B&E investigations never resulted in an arrest, let alone recovering the stolen goods. Nothing against my mom's investigative skills—she was great. Burglars were simply difficult to catch.

But something Dani said caught my attention.

"Did you say you were at the brewery late last night?" I asked.

She nodded. "Super late. Ray, Johnny, and I had to finish the new batches, and because we're doing more brews than ever, it's taking longer." She made a sour face. "Of course, Johnny made an excuse to leave early."

Johnny Boudreau, the other assistant brewer and bartender.

"But you didn't notice anything unusual when you left?"

Dani shook her head. "No, nothing. Ray went home. I cleaned up and then locked the Breeze. It was a normal night." She looked over my shoulder. Then down at her wristwatch. "I'd better get going. I want to talk to Ray and see if I can be helpful. Probably need to talk to your mom, too. And then we'll have to get started on new batches right away. I don't know how we'll catch up..."

She hurried off, heading in the direction I'd come from.

It was time for me to hurry, too, or I wouldn't meet my deadline. The story I was working on—all about the renovations at St. Gerontius Retirement Community—needed rewriting because of unexpected delays to construction, plus I had a short one about a new food truck appearing on Allington's shopping street, Peony Lane.

But as I hurried to work, my mind was on the Breeze and the burglary story. Would the press coverage hurt Ray and Roxie's business? I didn't think so. In fact, if I could get the burglary story out quickly, it might help them. My hope was it would have a positive effect—Allingtonians would visit the Breeze in a show of support. Because no one liked it when a local business suffered, right?

My mind flashed back to Dani.

When she'd wondered aloud who might tamper with

the fermentation, was there a moment when she'd hesitated? Like she'd thought of someone? Or was that just my
imagination?

4

T*he Allington Gazette* occupied an old firehouse with tall ceilings that amplified the click-clack-clack of my dad's typewriter.

I strode down the long aisle between desks, a sense of purpose egging me on. I was going to write a zinger of a story on the Breeze and rally everyone in town to support the business.

The desks were all empty, except for a vintage typewriter sitting on each, as if this were a museum and not a functioning local newspaper. My dad's stubborn commitment to analog technology meant that everyone at *The Gazette* had to type their articles on a manual machine before handing it over to him.

Everyone meant me. Since I was the only reporter.

I plonked down at my desk across from Dad's. My candy red Royal Quiet de Luxe awaited me. So did the laptop next to it. We didn't operate entirely in the past.

Dad lifted a hand in greeting and continued to type with the other, hammering down the keys. Clack-clack-clack. His typewriter was a teal green Olivetti Studio 44. He loved it the way some men love their cars, regularly cleaning it, oiling it, and, when he thought I wasn't listening, whispering affirmations to it.

"I've got news," I said.

"That's our business," he said, and his typewriter went ding and he hit the return lever, so the carriage slid into place for the next line. It was a pleasing sound. Even I had to admit that.

He leaned back, folded his hands over his ample belly, and smiled. With his big white beard and fisherman's sweater, he looked like a jolly version of Ernest Hemingway.

He said, "So, tell me, what's the breaking news?"

I told him about the discovery Ray and I had made. As my story progressed, my dad's smile vanished and his face fell. He sat up.

"That's awful." He reached for the phone on his desk. An old phone with a rotary dial, of course. As he spun the dial, and it made a quick clicking sound, he said, "I'm calling in the cavalry."

Calling in the cavalry meant phoning my siblings, Amy, Joy, and Scottie. One at a time, he told them to drop their plans for dinner and join us at the Breeze. It was time for the family to show its support. I couldn't hear the responses at the other end, but I knew Amy would quietly agree. Joy would enthusiastically voice her support and insist on bringing cake. And Scottie, Dad's last call, would complain about how this would disrupt his day.

Dad said, "Yes, I know entrepreneurs are busy, Scottie. But fortunately they're also flexible. And since you still live at home at Broadstairs House—"

Apparently, Scottie cut him off.

Dad listened, and then said, "Yes, you're right—Joy and Park also live at home. Which is why I happen to know what you've all got planned tonight. Dinner. So, I'll see you at the Breeze."

Dad dropped the phone receiver into its cradle and smiled at me again. "Now we have to write some articles lickety-split, and get the next edition of The Gazette ready for publication tomorrow, so we can head to the Breeze for dinner in—" He checked his wristwatch. "—eight hours."

I gave him a thumbs up. "Got it."

"And Park," he said. "I know the burglary's a big story for us. I know you want to help Roxie and Ray, and I love you for it. But you've got to finish the other articles first. Those stories are just as important to someone as the one about the Breeze. Got it?"

"Got it," I said with less enthusiasm.

We got working. The firehouse filled with the click-clack-clack of our typewriters. This was so different from my experience in the big city, where I'd worked for a national newspaper. Briefly. Before getting laid off. That was when I'd moved back to Allington, and to my surprise, discovered that it was where I belonged.

Including at *The Gazette*.

My dad's approach to running a paper was quirky. It wasn't for everyone. But I'd realized with time, I enjoyed it. It felt good. It felt like home.

After a few fact-checking phone calls, I finished the draft of the story about the St. Gerontius Retirement Community, handed the sheets of paper to Dad. Then fed another sheet into my typewriter and, glancing at my notes in my note-book, started typing the story about the new food truck on Peony Lane.

My phone pinged. A message from my Aunt Lil, Mom's eccentric sister:

Heard about the Breeze. Can't say I'm surprised. Saturn is retrograde in Pisces, so there you have it. The dark clouds of misfortune are gathering. See you for dinner. XO.

"Hey, Dad," I said. "Did you call Aunt Lil?"

He smiled. "Let me guess—she's coming to dinner?" He shrugged. "I didn't, and I doubt your mom called her, either. You know your aunt. Her star chart or tea leaves probably told her we'd be meeting as a family. Somehow she always knows."

Aunt Lil could be nutty at times, and yet she somehow knew things without anyone telling her. Like she had a sixth sense. Either that or she picked up on town gossip faster than anyone else. After all, the Allington grapevine did run straight through her hotel, the Lakeview Inn.

I went out to get us falafel wraps from the new food truck on Peony Lane, which gave more material for the story. But I also used it as an opportunity to talk to the owner about the Middle Eastern food he served, and how he transitioned from working in a restaurant to starting his own food truck.

Back at The Gazette, Dad and I ate our falafel wraps—which were delicious—and then he handed me my St. Gerontius story back with red pen marks in a few places. I finished the food truck draft and dropped it on his desk. Then scanned my St. Gerontius draft on the flatbed scanner and opened my laptop to finish it. Dad's commitment to analog only went so far.

I stretched, and my spine popped. Now it was time to dig into the burglary story.

First, I called Deputy Douglas.

"Hi, Parker," he said. He was chewing. I'd caught him on his lunch break. "You looking for your mom?"

"I'm looking for information about the burglary at the Breeze."

"Oh, jeez. You know I'm not at liberty to discuss ongoing...see the thing is, last time I told you stuff, well, I know your mom wouldn't want—oh. That's why you called me, and not your mom."

"Mom will fill me in, anyway. You know that."

A scratching sound on the end of the line. He was scratching his face, one of his many nervous gestures. He said, "Gee, I don't know what I can tell you."

Hemming and hawing were Deputy Douglas's specialty.

"Tell me anything you want," I said. "Even better, tell me everything you know."

"I can't. Not that I won't. I mean—" He sighed. Even he found his own hemming and hawing exhausting. "I don't know what I can tell you. Because there's nothing much to tell. We've come up with so little."

He detailed the evidence so far, which Ray and I had already discovered together. I thanked Deputy Douglas and hung up. This was bad news for the story. It might not have enough meat on the bone to merit a front-page placement. Which meant less exposure for the Breeze. And that meant less support from our town.

I rolled a fresh sheet of paper into my Royal Quiet de Luxe. If the burglary mostly remained a mystery, there was nothing I could do about it. Just write my story and hope for the best.

I started typing.

5

We finished later than planned and raced out to get down to the Breeze for dinner.

As we hurried along the docks, I noticed the soon-to-open wine bar now had a sign in the window:

> *Grand opening on Saturday:*
> *The Lakeview Wine Bar.*
> *The Best Food and Drink in Allington.*

"That's news, too," Dad said. "Lester Huxley's new wine bar. I'd better be there for the grand opening on behalf of *The Gazette*—and you know I never say no to a little wine tasting."

I frowned. Nobody owned the rights to "Lakeview," and since a wine bar on the docks did have a good view of the lake, the name wasn't exactly false advertising. Still. Everyone in town referred to Aunt Lil's place as "The Lakeview." Did the wine bar owner deliberately pick a name that was already popular in town?

And as we neared the Breeze, another thought struck me.

A wine bar—and one serving food—just a stone's throw from my brother's restaurant and bar. Was this direct competition?

More pressure on Ray and Roxie to catch up. This wasn't just news—it was bad news.

By the time Dad and I opened the door to the Breeze, I was convinced the business was in a downward spiral. The place would be a ghost town. Ray and Roxie would be boxing up things and getting ready to turn off the lights and file for bankruptcy.

I'd painted a pretty bleak picture in my mind.

But as soon as I stepped inside, I saw I was wrong. Wonderfully wrong. Every table and booth was occupied. The bar was crowded. Between the music and the many voices, I had to raise my voice to talk to Dad.

"What's going on?"

Dad shrugged. "Looks like a party."

"Hey, Dad, Park—over here!"

Across the restaurant, Scottie was waving at us from a booth. Dad and I wove through the crowd.

"Come on," Scottie said. He was wearing an I-love-Allington cap, one of the souvenirs he sold at his ice cream shop. "Squeeze in."

"Lucky thing you got here early," Dad said. "Or we wouldn't have found a place to sit. What in the world is going on?"

Joy smiled. Her smile lit up her face. "After you called, I told a few folks at Cafe Larke. Now half of Allington's come to show their support."

Joy's cafe was located on the corner of Peony Lane and Main

Street, and it was Allington's most popular coffee shop. Not least because of Joy's amazing cakes and cookies. At Cafe Larke, carrot-cake haters became converts. Dieters surrendered and ordered fudge brownies. And patisserie snobs forgot to turn their noses up as soon as they got a whiff of the cinnamon rolls.

Joy also ran the nearby yoga studio, Pure Joy. Maybe to balance out the cake eating. Yin-yang.

Amy nodded. "I also sent word out to the church community, encouraging anyone who felt moved by the incident to come."

She was the pastor at Shepherd's Gate Church. A word from her would've inspired many to change their evening plans. Her congregation—heck, most of town—respected her for her quiet, hardworking devotion to Allington's well-being, spiritual and otherwise.

"Of course, Ray and Roxie's friends spread the news, too," Joy said. "And you know how many people they know."

I looked around. "Where's Mom?"

"Ray said she finished fingerprinting and all that, and then had to go to the station to catalog the evidence and write a report," Scottie said.

I craned my neck, scanning the crowd. Through them, I could see Ray and Roxie behind the bar. I excused myself and headed over to say hello.

"Ah, my favorite niece."

At the bar, Aunt Lil draped herself across a stool in a voluminous paisley muumuu. Her bangles and half a dozen necklaces with talismans and crystals tinkled like a wind chime as she moved. And made me dizzy to look at.

"Darling Parker," she said, and she rummaged in her big, floppy shoulder bag and brought out a crystal wand. Selenite, it was called. Or moonstone. And she proceeded to wave it all around me. This was a familiar ritual—the cleansing of my aura—and I waited until she was done.

"You're welcome." With a dramatic sigh, she tucked the wand back into her bag. "That aura of yours—well, all I can say is you've let yourself go."

As she talked, I noticed the guy behind her was leaning forward on the bar, talking enthusiastically to Ray.

"So, yeah, draft is where it's at. But my regulars love bottled beer, too. And you know the drinking habits at my place are a little different because I don't serve food. Plus, I stay open so late."

He was a young guy with unruly hair and a scraggly beard. Vaguely familiar. He wore a flannel shirt with a red-and-black pattern. My brother Ray was nodding, listening patiently.

I frowned. Took another look at the guy, and then at Ray.

Ray sported a beard, too, though more well-grown and groomed. He also wore the same kind of flannel shirt with a red-and-black pattern. In a strange way, the two looked alike.

I leaned close to Aunt Lil and whispered, "Who is that guy?"

Aunt Lil leaned close and peeked back over her shoulder. She loved whispering. Next to loud dramatic proclamations, it was her favorite thing.

"That's Wally. Wally Wareham."

"Oh," I said, remembering him from high school as a little daredevil with a skateboard.

"Oh, indeed. He's a Leo." Aunt Lil raised an eyebrow. When I didn't react, she let out a huff of irritation. "That means he looks for recognition. He's drawn to charismatic leaders." She jerked her head toward Ray.

I let out a single, incredulous laugh. My big brother, a charismatic leader? Oh, come on.

"But, of course," Aunt Lil added, "the desire for attention and admiration, even love, can overpower a Leo's trustworthiness. Keep an eye on him. He may be a shapeshifter."

"A shapeshifter?"

"Besides," she added, ignoring my question, "with Saturn retrograde in Pisces, the Leo's dreams can become cosmic portals. He ignores them at his own peril. And ours."

She turned abruptly, swiveling on her barstool, and pointing a finger at Wally.

"Don't ignore your dreams, young man."

"Oh, I won't, Miss Lil," he said with a grin, completely unfazed. Most people in Allington were used to my Aunt Lil. "I'm living my dream. Speaking of which, Ray, I've gotta go. That bar won't open itself. See ya."

"See you later, Wally," Ray said.

We watched him go. As we did, Roxie joined us at the bar and stared off at Wally. The front door shut behind him. Roxie, leaning against the bar, frowned.

"I don't like that kid," she said, and her intensity surprised me.

Ray was surprised, too. "Roxie, come on. He's a nice kid."

"He's up to something. I can smell it a mile away."

"Well," Aunt Lil said, crossing her arms, eyeing me with a satisfied smile on her face. "Didn't I tell you so?"

6

"You're worrying about nothing," Ray told Roxie. "The only thing we have to worry about is whether we can keep up with all this business. I mean, with the destruction of the beer, how're we going to serve all these people?"

He reached for a clean pint glass. She took the glass from him and reached around to pull the nearest draft handle. Beer gushed into it. He grabbed another glass. Roxie and Ray moved around each other like well-choreographed dancers. As if they knew exactly what the other person needed.

Roxie said, "Wally's been hanging around the Breeze for days, asking you a million questions. Don't you think it's a little much? A little suspicious?"

Ray shrugged. "He runs a bar. I run a bar. It's normal."

"God help me," Roxie said with a sigh. "Sometimes you can be such a *man*."

Ray poked her, playfully. "Hey, how come *man* sounds like an insult?"

"Sorry." Roxie quirked a smile. She poked him back. "But sometimes you can be so obtuse."

"I love it when you use fancy words."

Roxie rolled her eyes at him and tossed her long, brown ponytail over her shoulder. She began to place full glasses with beer on a tray.

If Ray inspired fanboying in Wally, Roxie was no slouch, either. She was the kind of woman a teenage girl might fangirl over. Kind and strong and good-looking. And she was the brains behind the Breeze's business operations.

Ray had lucked out.

Today, she wore jeans and a polka-dot blouse with black dots. No doubt in imitation of Wimsey, their Dalmatian.

"Let me simplify it for you, my dear," she said. "Wally's not just fanboying. He's obsessed. And you just think he's being nice. I mean, he spends all his spare time hanging out at the Breeze. And then there's the name of his bar, for goodness' sake."

"What's with the name?" I asked.

"Zephyr Bar," Roxie said, giving me a raised eyebrow.

I looked at Ray, who shrugged.

Roxie smiled at me, expecting me to react.

I said, "I don't get it."

Aunt Lil nudged me. "Zephyr. As in 'a light breeze.'"

"Oh. Now I get it. He basically named his bar 'The Breeze.'" It was my turn to raise an eyebrow. And I turned to my brother. "Ray, come on. Roxie's right. Wally's obsessed."

Ray shook his head and walked down the bar to tend to another customer. "You're all overanalyzing this."

I called after him: "Or you're not analyzing it enough."

Aunt Lil said, "It fits with his star sign. He's a Cancer. So, now is a good time for growth and reassessment. And with

Saturn—" She cut herself off. "By the way, isn't his birthday next week?"

"Shh..." Roxie said, motioning for her to keep her voice down. "I'll talk to you about that later. I want to surprise him."

"Oh, wonderful," Aunt Lil said. "I love surprises. Although, naturally, nothing's a true surprise if you follow the stars."

Roxie hoisted up the tray with pints of beer and headed over to a table to deliver them.

Down the other end of the bar, a woman leaned across the counter to talk to Ray. Her hair was a bold black, with a hint of purple. Obviously dyed. She wore purple nail polish and dark purple lipstick. Together with her black turtle-neck, her style suggested a hint of goth.

I couldn't hear what she said. The voices and music in the bar were too loud, and they were too far away. But she leaned as close as she could to Ray and put a hand on his arm. Her eyes were large, the concern obvious on her face. Head cocked to the side. Even at a distance, I could read her body language: she was comforting him.

I got busy talking to Aunt Lil, asking her about business at the Lakeview Inn. The inn had gone through a quiet period, but now business was picking up. Which she'd anticipated. The alignment of the planets suggested that, after a time of difficulty, prosperity would return.

I nodded. Roughly, Aunt Lil's cosmic interpretations conveniently fit with the annual influx of tourists to Alling-ton. The good times were, indeed, ahead: more tourists would soon be coming to Allington. Which meant more business for everyone—from Cafe Larke to the Breeze. And what was good for Allington was good for my family.

Roxie returned to the bar with the empty tray, just as a

big, beefy guy came hurrying out of the door to the brewery, a backpack slung over his shoulder. Head down. Eyes low. As if he didn't want to be seen.

It was Johnny Boudreau, the Breeze's second assistant brewer and bartender. Dani's colleague. The restaurant had a larger staff, with servers working shifts, and Roxie and Ray hiring teens during peak season in summer. But only three people worked in the brewery: Ray, Dani, and Johnny.

Johnny's head was square, his jaw as solid as a brick, and his crewcut only accentuated the squareness. He looked like he lifted weights, his muscles straining his t-shirt. On his left bicep, a tattoo of a heart encased a D in gothic lettering. In a more modern font over that D, it said, "Grandma."

Roxie stepped out from the bar, blocking his path. "Whoa there, Johnny. Where are you off to?" She looked at her wristwatch. "A little early to call it quits, isn't it? Did Ray approve this?"

"I've got someplace to be, all right?" he snapped. "Anyway, the brewery team worked overtime last night."

"The team did," Roxie acknowledged. "Although Dani says you left early."

Johnny clenched his jaw. "Dani should mind her own business."

"And you should mind yours, Johnny." Roxie took a deep breath. She softened her voice. But it still had an edge to it. "Is there a problem with your schedule? Because this is becoming a regular thing—you sneaking off early and leaving others to finish the work. Do we need to talk about changing your responsibilities?"

"No," he said.

"All right. Then please stick to your work schedule."

Johnny grumbled. It was almost like a rumble. Like distant thunder. He clenched his fists. Lightning flashed in his eyes, and for a second, I worried he'd take a swing at Roxie. But Roxie stood her ground, staring him down.

He murmured something about not needing to be told what to do. Then swiveled around and stomped back to the brewery door. He slammed it behind him, loud enough to carry over the din in the bar and restaurant, and a few customers looked up.

Roxie shook her head. "That guy's been trouble from day one..."

Phew. That was close. The confrontation left me with a tingling sensation in my fingertips. My shoulders, without my knowledge, had tensed, and I forced myself to relax them.

Aunt Lil gave me a look. She didn't say anything. She didn't need to.

I was beginning to believe she might be right about Saturn and Pisces and the dark clouds of misfortune. Trouble definitely seemed to be brewing.

7

"Please, no more—I'm dying," Scottie said. He leaned back and put one hand on his belly as he let out a long breath. "One more bite and, I swear, I'll explode."

Joy had brought a massive Tupperware for dessert. Inside were brownies. Lots of brownies. And after a hearty dinner of Breeze burgers, fries, and salads, washed down with beer, we'd all indulged in a dessert that was as big as the main course.

Joy's fudge brownies were so fudgy, each bite stuck to my teeth. Thankfully, the vanilla ice cream—courtesy of Scottie's ice cream shop—helped dislodge the cake. That was my excuse for heaping more scoops onto my plate. I was really doing my dentist a favor.

By the time I finished, my stomach was crying for mercy. Everyone else looked just as stuffed.

Mom, still in her uniform, had undone a few buttons. "You've outdone yourself, Joy."

"And the combination with Scottie's ice cream..." Dad shook his head, smiling. "A dream come true."

We were sitting in the booth at the Breeze. Outside, night had fallen. The restaurant had emptied of other customers. It was a weeknight, so most folks left after dinner. But the Lee family had dug in for the long haul—we'd close the place down.

The only person who'd left early was Aunt Lil—she had a hotel to run, after all.

Ray and Roxie had joined the rest of the family for dinner. Then returned to work. Occasionally, one of us would jump up and join them, helping the servers clear tables or gather empty glasses for the bar. Then sit back down with the rest of the family and continue the banter.

Now, food drunk, we slowly levered ourselves off the leatherette seat in the booth and got busy stacking chairs on the tables, preparing for closing time.

The door to the brewery opened.

"I'm off," Johnny Boudreau called out, rushing toward the exit. "See you tomorrow."

Ray checked his watch and frowned. "All right, Johnny. See you tomorrow."

The front door shut behind Johnny.

Roxie nudged Ray. "Half an hour early."

"Well, it's better than yesterday when he left two hours early."

"You're too nice to him, and you know that Dani ends up picking up the slack. That's not fair."

Ray ran a hand through his hair and sighed. "Yeah, I know. In fact, I'm going out back to the brewery to help her with the new batches. She and Johnny cleaned the tanks, and we started over. We should be ready to ferment tomorrow." He crossed his fingers. "If all goes well."

Roxie looked at the time again and cursed. "I'm late to pick up Wimsey."

"You go," Ray said, and leaned close and gave her a kiss. "We'll finish up here."

Roxie hurried out.

I picked up a chair and placed it upside down on a table. My limbs felt heavy, like I was carrying around lead weights. Maybe that last heaping of ice cream had been a mistake.

After the chairs were off the floor, I got to work sweeping. Amy and Joy worked in the bar, stacking glasses. Scottie, Mom, and Dad wiped down the booths.

Together, we prepared the Breeze for another day of business. This was what we did as a family: we helped each other. When Amy had fundraisers at church, we showed up to spin the lucky number wheel, manage the ring toss competition, or sell cotton candy. We bought our coffee and cake at Joy's Cafe Larke, and if anyone ever suggested to meet for coffee, we knew which place we'd suggest. And, of course, we indulged in ice cream at Scottie's shop—and not just in summer.

Needless to say, everyone read *The Gazette*.

Ray insisted that Dani go home, and after telling her three times to get some sleep, she finally relented.

"See you tomorrow," she said, giving me a big smile before slipping out the door.

Soon, Amy said her goodbyes, too, and headed home. Then Mom, Dad, Joy, and Scottie left together, all returning to Broadstairs House, the old Victorian house we lived in together. I was the only one from the Broadstairs crew that stuck around.

"I thought you were going home with Mom and Dad," Ray said to me.

I shrugged. "I might as well make myself useful."

The truth was that Aunt Lil's weird talk about dark

clouds of misfortune sat like a rock in my stomach (it wasn't just the brownies). If I went home, I'd lay awake, worrying about something bad happening.

Ray switched off the lights in the bar. Then the restaurant. We left through the front door. A locksmith had been by to install a new lock. The security camera was fixed. Hopefully, no one would attempt another break-in.

After Ray had locked the door, I lingered outside the Breeze. Looking up and down along the docks. No signs of any suspicious characters. Anyway, what were the chances that a burglar would strike again so soon?

"You coming?" Ray said. "I'll drive you home."

We ambled down along the docks. There was a full moon tonight. It bathed Lake Allington in silver.

We turned the corner and stepped off the docks and came to Main Street. Ray led me toward the municipal parking lot where his car was parked. But something made me hang back again.

That uneasy feeling in the pit of my stomach. It got heavier. I gazed up at the night sky. The stars seemed infinite tonight, and some of them were surely planets.

I sighed. Aunt Lil was always talking about planets being misaligned—or seeing trouble in tea leaves. Was there any truth to it? I didn't know. But I knew this: I didn't like leaving the Breeze behind tonight.

"Go home," I told Ray. "It's a beautiful night. I don't mind walking."

"You sure?"

I nodded.

He gave me a big bear hug. "Thanks for everything today."

I turned on my heels and hurried back to the docks.

Ray's hug had loosened something in me. The uneasy feeling felt a little less uneasy. Maybe I was making too much of it.

Still, it couldn't hurt to take one last look...

I turned onto the docks. The water squelched in the darkness below. And the moonlight shone down on the scene in front of me like stage lights: Down by the big brick building occupied by the Breeze, a shadowy figure loped along the dock.

A crowbar in his hand.

My heart flew into my throat. The burglar!

I broke into a run.

Stop, I silently screamed. But actually yelling might scare him.

My sneakers slapped the boards of the dock.

The shadow stopped and looked up. Must've heard me.

The crowbar clattered to the boards of the dock.

He turned and bolted.

"Stop!" I yelled.

At the end of the dock, just past Scottie's ice cream shop, he swung down a ladder.

I sprinted. Desperate to catch up.

A night bird cried out, his voice carrying across the lake. My shoes slapped the boards. Up ahead, something splashed in the water.

I panted and cursed. Why'd he have to hear me coming? Why couldn't I be closer already?

I reached the end and came to a stop. I bent over, hands on my knees, panting, trying to catch my breath. Out on the lake, the man hauled at the oars of his rowboat. The oars slapped the water. No master rower. But he was good enough to get the boat moving.

Still, by the light of the bright moon, I recognized his face.

"Gotcha," I muttered, smiling to myself. I dug out my phone and hit speed dial. "Hey, Mom. Guess who I saw trying to break into the Breeze..."

8

The next day, Thursday, I stopped by the Breeze in the afternoon. I could hardly wait to tell Ray what I'd discovered last night. But getting The Gazette to press turned out to take longer than usual that morning, and by the time Dad and I were done, it was past lunch.

I burst through the door to the Breeze, expecting to find Ray at the bar. But Roxie stood behind the counter. For a second, I assumed Ray must be in the back, in the brewery. Then I saw him.

He was sitting in a booth in the back of the restaurant. Across from the woman with the purple lipstick. He was holding a sheet of paper as he talked to her and she was nodding seriously, her hands folded on the table between them.

I leaned against the bar. Roxie was wiping down the counter.

"That almost looks like a job interview," I said, gesturing toward Ray and the woman with purple lipstick.

"That's because it is a job interview. If all goes well, Sandra Pyke will be our new bartender and server."

I did a double take, staring at the woman sitting across from Ray.

"No way. That's Sandra Pyke? I didn't recognize her without the heavy black mascara, steel-plated boots, and three nose rings."

"She's changed a lot since her high-school goth metal days."

"But Roxie—" I dropped my voice. Not sure how to put this. "—is Sandra a good fit? I mean, for the Breeze?"

Roxie lifted an eyebrow. "Just say it, Park."

"All right, then. Is hiring one of Ray's ex-girlfriends really a good idea?"

"They dated a long time ago."

"She was pretty obsessed with him."

"And I hear she's pretty obsessed with a new guy." Roxie cocked her head, giving me a sympathetic smile. It made me feel a little crazy. Like I was spinning nutty conspiracy theories. And maybe I was. "Don't worry, Park. Sandra's cool."

Roxie offered me a drink while I waited, and I had a raspberry spritzer with a sprig of mint. My addiction to raspberry spritzers was seasonal. As the weather got warmer, I began to crave them. Then, a couple weeks before Halloween, they'd stop tasting as good, and I'd switch to apple ciders.

After a while, Ray came to the bar. Sandra headed for the restrooms.

"So?" Roxie said.

Ray gave a thumbs up. "She'll be great. Did you know she attended bartending school?"

"Then let's move forward with her."

"Guys, are you sure about this?" I said. "There must be a business book that says hiring ex-girlfriends is a no-no."

"Yeah, right along with don't start a business with your spouse," Roxie said.

Ray smiled. "Park, whatever happened between me and Sandra—that's ancient history. She and I have been friends for more years than we dated. I trust her. She's one of the most reliable people I know. I mean, back when I was in a dark place, she was a rock for me."

"Back when you dated, you mean?"

"Yeah, all right, back when we dated. But also later. After we broke up, she helped me. Not every ex does that. She's the kind of person who cares about her friends. Really cares. We need that at the Breeze."

I recognized that as a subtle reference to Johnny Boudreau. Who obviously didn't care, and it was driving Ray and Roxie crazy.

"Besides, she's got a fiancé," Ray added. "Otherwise, sure, I might have more reservations about it. But the two of them are super serious. As soon as he gets back from his deployment, they're getting hitched."

"He's in the military?"

Ray nodded. "Navy. Stationed somewhere in the Middle East."

I gave a low whistle. "Long-distance relationship."

"That's why she's back in Allington," Roxie said. "She told me she'd rather be around friends and family than sit in San Diego waiting for him to come home."

Dani came through the brewery door. She was wearing a face mask. As she came to the bar, she slipped it off and ran the back of a hand across her forehead.

"You look like you could use a cold drink," Roxie said.

Dani nodded. "Yeah, and a helping hand. Have you seen Johnny?"

"I thought he was back there with you."

"Nope. He went out for lunch and hasn't come back."

Roxie cursed. "I'd better give him a call."

She dug out her phone and wandered down the bar.

Dani made herself a seltzer with lots of ice. Sandra, returning from the restrooms, joined us at the bar. When Dani saw her, she gave Sandra a big smile.

"Hey, roomie. How did it go?"

"Great." Sandra glanced over at Ray. "At least I think so."

Ray nodded and smiled. "Agree. You did great. In fact, Roxie and I agree: we'd like to offer you the position, if you're interested."

Sandra beamed. "Interested? You better believe it. Working at the Breeze is a dream gig. This is like the heart of Allington. What could be better?"

"That's what we're looking for—that passion for the Breeze," Ray said, nodding. Again, a subtle critique of Johnny. "Can you start on Monday?"

Sandra nodded. "Thanks, Ray."

Dani grinned and high-fived Sandra. I got the sense the two of them were good friends. And didn't Dani call Sandra her *roomie*?

I said, "Do you two live together?"

Dani nodded. "My old roommate bailed on me, and I was desperate. Then Sandra came back to Allington. It was perfect timing for me."

Sandra nudged Dani. "It was perfect timing for *me*."

"Honestly, Sandra, if I hadn't bumped into you at the volunteer orientation at the center, I would've had to break the lease. I would've been heartbroken."

"I kinda insisted on sitting with you at lunch. And then insisted on your joining me on my shift."

Dani laughed. "You did. You totally recruited me."

The two of them started talking about their own stuff—

swapping stories about this volunteer work they did—and I turned to Ray, tugging at his sleeve. He slipped onto a stool and gave me his full attention.

"You've got something to tell me," he said, studying me. "And it's killing you to keep it a secret."

"Yes!" I grinned. "So, after we said goodbye last night, I came back to the Breeze. And you'll never guess who I saw..."

I tapped my fingers on the edge of the bar, imitating a drumroll.

"Iggy Huxley," Ray said.

I stopped my drumroll. Gaped at my brother.

He shrugged. "Mom told me last night. Besides, it's a day later. By now, Aunt Lil's already told half of Allington." He put a hand on my shoulder, a gesture of sympathy. "Next time, kiddo, call me right after the big discovery. Then you can give me a drumroll."

"Drumrolls don't work over the phone."

"Anyway," he said, "did Mom tell you about the fingerprints?"

I threw up my hands. "No. She did not tell me about the fingerprints. Does all of Allington know this, too?"

"They match ones on record for one Ignatius Huxley."

I took a deep breath and calmed down. "All right. So we've got our burglar?"

"Looks like it."

"Case closed?"

"If Mom can track him down."

Dani broke off from the conversation she was having with Sandra. "Track who down?"

"Iggy Huxley," Ray said. "You know him? Long, stringy hair. Skinny. Looks undernourished."

"The homeless guy?" Dani said.

"Dani," Sandra said. "Remember. We prefer *unhoused*."

Dani nodded. "I know him. I mean, I've seen him around. He's in and out of rehab."

I said to Ray, "Which means Mom will know all his usual haunts. She'll track him down."

Ray nodded. "And if anyone can get the truth out of Iggy about why he sabotaged our batch of beer, it's Mom."

"Wait, Iggy did that?" Dani said, her jaw dropping.

Sandra put a hand to her heart. "Oh, no. And from what I heard, he was genuinely trying to clean up…"

Roxie rejoined us, and Ray filled her in on hiring Sandra. Then the conversation shifted from Iggy to what a wonderful addition to the team Sandra would make. Sandra brushed off the compliments with modesty, and then gushed about the Breeze.

"This is so great," Dani said.

She seemed as excited as Sandra about the job.

I checked the time. I had one last article to write today. A guy who caught a 12-pound burbot. Not a state record, but a first for Allington.

I drained my raspberry spritzer and slipped off the stool. Time to get back to work. I wanted to clear my desk, so I was ready for when Mom called later today to confirm she'd arrested Iggy.

As I left the Breeze, I was thinking of what a solid little story it would make—with all the strings neatly tied up. Iggy Huxley caught red-handed.

Huxley.

Didn't I hear that name recently, but in a different context?

9

Mom didn't find Iggy that Thursday. And Friday —despite my checking my phone for new messages every 3 minutes—passed without an arrest, too.

By Saturday, Mom told me to stop calling and texting her.

"I'll let you and your dad know when I've got news to share." I was sitting at my desk at *The Gazette*. It was the third time I'd called her that afternoon. I didn't even want to count the amount of text messages.

"Don't worry," she said. "Iggy's probably hiding out somewhere in the woods. He's never left Allington in his life. I don't think he'll run. Sooner or later, he'll turn up."

"But what if—?"

She cut me off. "Park, sweetie, I know I usually involve you in investigations. But you'll just have to be patient. In the meantime, don't you have other work to do?"

"I do. The wine bar's grand opening is today."

"I thought your dad was writing that story."

"Yeah, but I might as well tag along."

Silence at the other end. On my end, only the sound of Dad click-clacking on his Olivetti.

Then Mom said, "And this has nothing to do with the break-in?"

"The break-in?" I snorted, trying to sound natural. "Why would it have anything to do with the break-in?"

"Because the wine bar is owned by Lester Huxley, Iggy's brother."

"Oh, sure. Dad did mention that. But in a small town like Allington, almost everyone you meet is related to someone else you know. I mean, look at our family. Besides, it can't hurt to learn more about Lester if I'm going to write a story about his brother."

"Just tread lightly, Park. Tread lightly."

"I'll be like a ballet dancer," I promised.

Later that afternoon, Dad packed up early to leave for the wine bar, and I prepared to do the same. We were halfway to the exit when the phone rang. The old rotary on Dad's desk. It was the official *Gazette* line, and people rarely called that number, since most folks knew my dad's cell or mine.

"Will you get that?" Dad said.

I jogged back to his desk, expecting the ringing to cut off at any moment. I picked up the receiver.

"*The Allington Gazette*, Parker Lee speaking."

"I know something," a voice said. A man's voice. Raspy and faint. Bad connection? Or bad vocal cords? Maybe a bit of both. He said, "I know something about the break-in at the Breeze, and I'll tell you for a thousand dollars."

I let out a laugh, a single bark. I couldn't help it. "You serious? A thousand bucks? This isn't *The National Enquirer*."

"Uh," the guy said. "How about five hundred?"

I sighed. "Iggy, how about you drop by and we can talk?"

Iggy cursed, confirming my guess that he was the mystery man.

"I'm not—"

He cursed again.

Click.

He'd hung up on me.

I put down the receiver. Then grabbed my cell phone and called Mom, filling her in.

"We'll find him," she said. "Don't worry. And in the interim, Park. Stay out of trouble."

"Of course. Don't I always?"

"I'll plead the Fifth on that."

On our way out of the old firehouse, I was thinking about Mom's warning. She was worried about my visit to the wine bar. Why would she warn me to tread lightly, stay out of trouble? Did she herself see a connection between Lester and Iggy and the break-in at the Breeze?

As Dad and I wandered down Main Street, heading toward the docks, I told him about the call from Iggy. We speculated about what information he could possibly want to sell about the break-in he himself did. Of course, he might be drunk and delusional. But something told me there was more to it than that.

"Do you know Lester Huxley?" I asked. "Iggy's brother?"

"Sure. He's a local business owner. He used to own a restaurant on Peony Lane. The Walrus, it was called. And he was a co-owner of that popular gym."

"Fab4Fitness?"

"That's the one. He briefly ran a cafe and bar, too. Down on the docks, in fact. But it didn't last long."

"Why not?"

Dad shrugged. "Lester's all hard edges. Not exactly lovable. But the real problem was that the cafe was nothing special. A small place with mediocre coffee and baked goods, uninspired sandwiches, and then a measly selection of wine and beer. All at a high price. Maybe there was too much competition, too. The Breeze is big, its interior is charming, and the view outside is great."

"And let's not forget Ray's beers," I said. "Nobody does beer like Ray."

Dad put an arm around my shoulders and gave me a squeeze. "You're a good sister."

As we turned onto the docks, I thought about Lester Huxley. The wine bar was Lester's second attempt to compete with the Breeze. According to Dad, he wasn't lovable. Did that mean he resented Ray and Roxie for their success? Enough to send his brother to sabotage the brewery?

Once Mom caught up with Iggy, we'd find out.

In the distance, someone was ambling along the dock, coming toward the wine bar from the far end. I knew that amble.

Oh, crap.

"Hey, isn't that Ray?" Dad said.

"Yeah, and he's heading to the grand opening."

"Oh." Dad's bushy eyebrows shot up. "Oh, dear."

10

The "Grand Opening" sign wasn't the only evidence of an event. A string of pennants hung over the entrance. Tables outside provided customers not only with seating in the fresh air but also with a stunning view of Lake Allington and the woods that ringed it. A server carried a tray with glasses of complementary wine. Another offered small ramekins with olive oil and hunks of bread for dipping. A crowd had already gathered to enjoy the free drinks and food. People engaged in loud conversation both inside and outside.

Dad stopped to say hello to people he recognized. I slipped past them and stepped inside the wine bar. The interior had a classy, atmospheric feel. A bar decorated with vintage posters from France and Italy. Walls lined with bottles. Old wine casks serving as small tables for two. Longer farmhouse tables for bigger parties.

At one of the casks stood a woman with a clipboard. A sign on the cask said, "Bartenders and servers wanted."

I looked around. Where had Ray gone? I didn't see him.

Maybe he got waylaid by a friend—or he was tucked away in a corner, hidden by the crowd.

It would be easy to miss him. The wine bar was packed with people. Half of Allington seemed to have turned up. Lots of familiar faces: Ashley from Cafe Larke talking to Balthazar of Balthazar Books and Manfred Hertz from the stationery store, Miranda Gottschall from Larke House and her wife, each sipping red wine and then swapping glasses to compare, and Sandra Pyke chatting with Wally Wareham, both drinking beer.

Beer. I didn't expect the wine bar to carry beer.

I picked up a laminated menu. Half a dozen wines on offer in each category: red, white, rose, and sparkling. Then a food menu leaning heavily on Mediterranean food, from tapas to meze. Plus, perennial favorites like burgers. But the big surprise was the beer selection: two dozen craft-brew beers. A sticker on the menu advertised surprisingly low prices.

Really, with that kind of selection, the place should be called a "wine and beer bar."

At the bar, my other brother, Scottie was talking to a bald man with a black mustache.

"So it's called Sugar Glider Brew," he was saying as I approached, "and it's an exclusive Australian brand. A fruity lager. It appeals to a much broader customer base than your ordinary lager."

I smiled to myself. For a while now, Scottie had been importing an obscure Australian beer, convinced that he was going to make millions distributing it in North America. I'd already heard him pitch the idea to several businesses, usually with no luck. Of course, Ray had agreed to carry Sugar Glider Brew at the Breeze. But that was more about family duty than a smart business move.

Scottie said, "I can get you set up right away. The tourists will love it. And I've got marketing materials and swag that—"

"Stop," the man said, holding up a hand. "I've heard enough."

Scottie grinned. "So you'll take it?"

"Absolutely not. It sounds awful."

"But, Lester—"

The man gestured at the wine bar around him. "Look at this place. It's classy. It's something you can't get down on the docks. Not like that glorified roadhouse your brother calls a restaurant and bar."

So this was Lester Huxley.

Scottie said, clearly taken aback, "But people love the Breeze."

"Because it's all they've got," Lester said. "If you live in Podunk, then Podunk Roadhouse probably seems like the Ritz. But Allington is evolving. Our town is growing up, and it deserves some adult food and drink. Speaking of which…"

He turned away from Scottie, grabbed a bottle of white wine, and filled a glass.

He said, "Mona—try this. You'll like it."

His back to Scottie.

I put a hand on my brother's shoulder.

"Better luck next time," I said.

He frowned. "Last week, he seemed so open to talking. He dropped by the ice cream shop and asked me all about Sugar Glider—and beers, in general. And I don't get why he's so dismissive of the Breeze now. When we talked the first time, he was super interested in the business, and how Ray selects his beers." Scottie frowned. "I bet he did that just to get information out of me."

I glanced over at Lester. He was talking to a woman

wearing a blue blazer and a pearl necklace. She sipped her wine and then pursed her lips, as if it helped her appreciate the flavor more.

"Like it, Mona?" Lester said.

"Love it," Mona said.

I'd seen this Mona somewhere before, but I wasn't sure where. Maybe church.

As I was trying to place her, Ray appeared out of the crowd. I bit my lip. Mom had warned me to tread lightly. But had she warned Ray?

As my brother approached Lester and Mona, it was as if I could feel the vibrations of his footsteps.

Lester's black eyebrows pressed into a frown.

"Hey, Mona, hi, Lester," Ray said, smiling and holding out a hand to shake Lester's. "Congratulations. The wine bar looks beautiful."

Lester left Ray hanging, refusing to shake.

"Thank you," Lester said. Cold as ice.

After a moment, Ray dropped his hand. His smile faltered. "Anyway," he said, more subdued now. "I just wanted to welcome you back to the neighborhood. It's great to have another bar on the block."

"Thank you," Lester repeated. Even colder.

Then silence. Lester said nothing. Ray, rubbing the back of his neck, looked uncomfortable. He said, "Well, good luck with it. Drop by the Breeze if you need anything."

Lester simply nodded this time, and Ray turned around and walked away. To her credit, the woman, Mona, looked embarrassed. She finished her wine and set the empty glass down.

"I have an appointment," she said. "Congratulations, Lester. Ray's right: the bar looks beautiful."

Lester frowned. Maybe at the way Mona had aligned herself with Ray. He muttered, "Thanks for coming."

Mona headed for the exit, glancing at Ray, who'd stopped to talk to a friend. For a moment, she hesitated. Then she went out, and nearly bumped into a guy coming in.

Thick as a brick. Thumping into the wine bar.

Ray looked up and saw him right after I did.

"Johnny," he said. "What're you doing here?"

Scottie nudged me and said, "Here comes trouble."

Scottie and I moved closer.

Johnny frowned. He glanced over at someone in the crowd, as if he'd come to talk to someone. But I couldn't make out who. Then he squared up to Ray.

He said, "I'm curious about Lester's wine bar. Like everyone else. Can't I take a break to come check it out?"

"Actually," Ray said, his frown as deep as Johnny's. "You can't. Someone needs to manage the bar."

"Dani can handle it."

"I need Dani in the back. I've asked her to stick exclusively to the brewery. The taproom is your responsibility."

Johnny mock-saluted Ray. "Yessir."

Then he turned around and, head down, stomped out of the wine bar.

Scottie and I joined Ray. Ray was taking deep breaths, his fists clenched. I rarely saw Ray lose his temper. He was pretty even-keeled, but Johnny got under his skin.

Johnny's experience as a brewer had been crucial for the Breeze's growth. But recently, he'd become more and more unreliable and rude. Ray had tried being patient and supportive, but again and again, Johnny had taken advantage of how relaxed my brother was. Ray had been too lenient. That was my brother's weakness: he didn't like confrontations.

I didn't think Johnny would change. Sooner or later, Ray would need to make a decision about him.

"Sooner or later—" I said.

"Yeah," Ray said, cutting me off. "I know. Sooner or later."

"Come on," Scottie said, putting a hand on Ray's shoulder. "Let's go back to the Breeze."

The three of us left. But before I stepped outside, I glanced over my shoulder.

Lester was watching us. His eyes hard and cold. His gaze sent a shiver down my spine. He didn't just resent Ray. He resented us all—the whole Lee family. Or was I just imagining that?

11

"What am I going to do with all these crates?"

Scottie took off his cap, ran a hand through his hair with a heavy sigh, and then put his hat back on. Inside Scottie's Ice Cream Shop, every available inch of floor space was covered in boxes. Each one bore a logo with a cute beady-eyed rodent with gliding wings. Kind of like a flying squirrel. Big letters on the boxes said, "Sugar Glider Brew: Australia's Sweetest Beer."

"I thought I'd be able to move more of them," Scottie said. "But I've only sold six cases so far. And I've got more coming."

"More?" I blurted. "Are you nuts? How many did you order?"

He grimaced. "There are about 500 cases stuck in customs right now."

"That's—" I searched for the right words. Nothing delicate came to mind. "—a crazy amount. Considering you don't have customers yet."

"I've got the Breeze," Scottie said.

"Because Ray's doing you a favor. Speaking of which." I

checked the time. It was Sunday morning, and I'd promised to help Scottie move some of the boxes to his storage room at the back before we went to church. "We'd better get started on this before—"

The door to the ice cream shop flew open. Ray filled the doorway, his eyes wide.

"Park, Scottie—" He was breathing heavily. Must've dashed over from the Breeze. "Come quick."

Then, without waiting for an answer, he spun around. His footsteps slapped the boards of the dock. Scottie and I exchanged glances, then bolted, too.

I took the lead. My sneakers hammering against the dock. The morning air cool against my face. In a moment, I reached the Breeze.

The door stood open. Once again, someone had forced their way inside. Splintered wood. Broken lock. I glanced up. This time, the burglar had been less patient with the camera. Smashing it rather than covering it. Must've used something like a baseball bat. The camera dangled on its wires.

Scottie caught up with me.

"Jeez," he said. "Not again."

"Come on. Let's find Ray."

The bar was empty. No sign of our brother. The cash register was closed. The bottles on the shelves behind the bar appeared to be lined up. All in order. Undisturbed.

I bit my lip. The brewery. The damage would be in the back. What had Iggy done this time?

I pulled open the door with the "danger" sign and Scottie and I hurried into the brewery. The vats in the front looked the same as always. Shiny. Clean. The tiled floor, too.

"Back here," Ray said.

He was standing by the fermentation tanks in the

section where the ceiling expanded upward. Near the metal walkway and its stairs.

At the bottom of the stairs lay a crumpled body.

Rumpled clothes. Scraggly hair tied into a ponytail. A crowbar by his right hand.

"Oh, man," Scottie said, grimacing at the sight.

Ray crouched down. Maybe to check his pulse. But there was no question—the pool of dark blood by Iggy's head confirmed it.

He was dead.

I stepped forward and put a hand on Ray's shoulder, restraining him. Because I knew just what Mom would say.

"Don't touch a thing. This is a crime scene."

12

Not a pew at Shepherd's Gate Church stood empty. As usual, my sister Amy's Sunday service attracted many people, and the Lee family never missed a sermon.

But today was different. Mom wasn't with us. She was down at the Breeze with Deputy Douglas, the county coroner, and the forensics team, cataloging and studying everything at the crime scene.

Dad sat next to me on the right. Joy was to my left, and then it was Scottie. Who wasn't paying attention but was instead reading another biography of a millionaire entrepreneur. And if I leaned forward, I could spot Ray and Roxie down at the end.

Ray and Roxie were holding hands, both looking grim. They didn't always come to church on Sunday––at least not both of them––unless they could find someone to watch Wimsey. Not because Amy had anything against dogs in her church. Right now, a woman across the aisle had a sheepdog lying at her feet. But Wimsey was an excitable Dalmatian. Whenever there were a lot of people, he got too excited. Especially around people he loved. If Roxie and Ray brought him, he was likely to charge up the nave, leap up on Amy in the middle of the sermon and knock her over, so he could shower her with his "kisses" to show how much he loved her. Delightful—but a little too disruptive.

So no Wimsey at church.

Amy stood in front of the congregation, a Bible in her hand. She didn't always read from the Bible. Even though she was a Christian pastor—or part of the Christian tradition, as she'd say—her service often referenced Buddhism or Hinduism or Islam or some other faith tradition. She believed that every tradition could teach us something about being better human beings and experiencing God's love.

Today, though, she quoted from Proverbs.

"*A heart at peace gives life to the body, but envy rots the bones.* Listen," she said. "We all feel envy. It's human. But what matters is what we do with that envy. Do we see our neighbor's success and envy it, and set out to destroy it? And risk destroying ourselves?" She paused. "Or do we see our neighbor's success and envy it, yet love our neighbor? Love can help us draw inspiration from another's success and emulate it. Love can help us create rather than destroy."

She gazed at us, appearing to recognize everyone in the church. She had a talent for seeing people, making them feel seen.

She said, "Love your neighbor, we're taught. So, does envy stand in opposition to love? I'm not so sure. In a way, envy is about love. A kind of unrequited love. Or love bent out of shape. We see someone's good fortune—their success in business, romance, or even conventional good looks—and somewhere inside us a voice asks, *Why does God love her more than me? Why? Why does he get what he wants? Why can't I be blessed with that, too?"*

She continued her sermon. But my mind went to Lester Huxley. Did he envy Roxie and Ray's success with the Breeze? Did he feel entitled to what Ray and Roxie—working so hard over so many years—had achieved with their restaurant, bar, and brewery? And if Lester did feel envy, was he using it as a source of inspiration to strive for his own success? Or did he want to destroy it?

"Rot takes time," Amy was saying. "Envy—and other perversions of love—can work on us slowly. Often unseen. Unnoticed. So, if you have 10 minutes later today, I urge you to take a quiet moment to sit and contemplate the line from Proverbs: *A heart at peace gives life to the body, but envy rots the bones.* What thing from your past might be festering inside you? What stops you from being at peace?"

She led us in prayer. We sang psalms. And through it all, my mind was on the break-in at the Breeze and the murder of Iggy Huxley.

After the service ended, the congregation got up. Some left, but many stayed for the coffee, tea, and cake that Amy always provided, courtesy of my other sister, Joy.

Joy had set up a table with coffee urns, thermoses with hot water for tea, and two trays: one with brownies, the other with cookies. The cookies were vegan. The brownies not. In fact, I had a brownie and guessed it must be about 69 percent butter. Yummy—but so rich, it took my breath away.

As I munched my brownie and sipped my coffee, Dad and I speculated about what had happened at the Breeze. I looked around for signs of Roxie and Ray. They stood at some distance, talking to Sandra. Nearby, Amy was talking to the woman I'd seen at the wine bar, Mona. And Scottie was in conversation with a guy who owned a restaurant on

Peony Lane. I could guess what they were talking about: Sugar Glider Brew. I silently wished my brother good luck.

After a while, he came over, looking disappointed.

"Another strike," he said with a sigh. Then he raised his hands and blew into them. "Maybe my breath isn't helping. Anyone got some gum?"

"I think I've got some," I said, and dug into my pocket.

But instead of a packet of gum, I found the weathered card with the half-legible prayer. The one I'd found near the Breeze after discovering Iggy's first break-in.

"Huh," I said to myself.

Leaving Scottie to find gum from someone else, I headed over to Amy. When I sensed a natural break in her conversation with Mona, I said, "Hey, sis. Great sermon. Can you tell me what this is?"

She studied the card. But just for an instant. She knew at once.

"That's the Serenity Prayer."

"The what?"

Mona jumped in. "The Serenity Prayer is used in a lot of twelve-step programs. Like Alcoholics Anonymous. In fact, a lot of the people we serve rely on it as a reminder during difficult times. For some, it's a constant companion. Can I see?" She came closer and peered at the card. "Oh, this is actually one of ours."

"One of yours?" I asked. "One of whose?"

"Concordia House."

That made sense. Concordia—not Concord. I knew of Concordia House. It was a recovery center and halfway house. Suddenly, the card took on a different meaning.

"Wait a minute, did Iggy Huxley come to Concordia?"

Mona frowned. "I can't talk about our patients."

Which, of course, confirmed that he did.

"I understand," I said. "But see, I found this card near the Breeze, and it might be important."

"Certainly someone who attended our programs could've carried the card," Mona said, clearly choosing her words carefully. She had that look on her face that people sometimes got talking to me—the just-realized-you-write-for-the-paper look. "Though a volunteer might carry the cards, too."

Amy, as if gently steering the conversation toward safer territory, said, "Ray used to volunteer at Concordia, didn't he?"

Mona smiled. "He sure did. And the Breeze still donates food and soft drinks."

Another connection to the Breeze. But did it mean anything? In a small town like Allington, everyone and everything was connected. More or less.

I flipped the card over. Did the weather ruin the card or had its owner worn it out? And if it belonged to Iggy, was it coincidence that he dropped it outside his brother's soon-to-open wine bar?

One thing was for sure: if it had belonged to Iggy, it was evidence in a murder investigation. Mom would want it.

13

Three cups of coffee—one for Mom, one for Dad, and one for me—stood steaming next to my candy red Royal Quiet de Luxe. Dad leaned back in his desk chair, which he'd wheeled close to us. Mom perched on my desk.

She said, "The killer struck Iggy with the crowbar. Death would've been instantaneous." She shook her head. "Poor guy. I've spent a couple of decades dealing with Iggy. Drunk and disorderly. B&Es. Petty theft. But when he finally checked into Concordia House, I was hoping he'd turned a corner."

"The Gazette will run a story on his life," Dad said. "Park, I want you to dig up as much as you can on Iggy. He was one of our own. Let's write a respectful profile of him."

"You got it," I said.

"But be careful, Park," Mom said. "Iggy was murdered for a reason, and the killer's still at large. We don't know what we're dealing with here."

"Poor Iggy," Dad said, shaking his head. "He was getting help. If only it had been enough."

"It clearly wasn't," Mom said. "Why else would he break into the Breeze?"

I said, "I bet someone convinced him to do it."

Mom nodded. "Agree. Iggy had no logical reason to sabotage the brewery. Stealing booze? Sure. Opening the cash register. OK. Classic relapse to bad habits. But sabotage?" She shook her head. "I don't see it."

"All right," Dad said. "So someone convinced him. But who?"

I stared across at Dad's desk. At the old phone. The call Iggy had made to *The Gazette* was about money. I bet I knew what he was selling. For the right price, he was going to reveal who paid him to sabotage the Breeze.

I shared my theory with Mom and Dad.

"But why turn on his employer?" Mom asked.

I shrugged. "Maybe he got greedy. He wanted more money and his employer wasn't willing to pay. After all, Iggy asked *The Gazette* to pay a thousand bucks for his story."

"Which we sure don't have," Dad said, smiling ruefully.

"Exactly. So maybe his employer didn't either."

"Or," Mom added, "his employer was simply unwilling to pay that much."

Either way, for the employer, Iggy had gone from being a valuable asset to becoming a liability. From employee to blackmailer.

I thought through what might've happened then. "So the killer sends Iggy for one more round of sabotage and then, once that's done—" I slammed my right fist into my left palm. "—*whack*."

I shuddered, thinking of poor Iggy's last moment in this life.

Mom said, "Except the sabotage didn't happen. The killer got to Iggy before he could reach the fermentation vats. You know the metal staircase to the walkway above? We found his fresh fingerprints at the very bottom of the railing. But not further up. He must've been about to climb the steps when the killer surprised him."

I frowned. That didn't make sense. "If the employer hired Iggy to do the sabotage," I said, "then why murder him before the job was done?"

"Maybe it wasn't the saboteur employer," Dad suggested. "Maybe it was someone else."

"Or it was the saboteur employer," Mom said. "But that person wanted to raise the stakes. After all, this murder has sabotaged the Breeze's business even more."

"How so?" I asked.

"If Iggy had ruined another batch of beer, it would've made Roxie and Ray's lives harder. But as it is..."

The realization struck me like a blow to the stomach.

"Oh, no," I groaned. "Don't tell me..."

Mom grimaced. "I'm sorry, but it's true. Since the Breeze is a crime scene, it's off limits. Closed for business."

ically centered-->

14

The next evening, Monday, people crowded around Lester's wine bar. Every table, whether inside or outside, was occupied, and wine and beer-sipping customers stood in clusters on the dock. With the Breeze closed, Lester's place was the only option if you wanted to grab a drink by the lake.

My sister Amy would probably say something about loving thy neighbor, while Joy would, joyfully, say that everything would be all right in the end, and that Lester deserved some blessings, too.

Which was why I was glad to have gone with Scottie.

He said, "What a jerk. He's taking full advantage of the Breeze being closed."

"Well, he's got a business to run," I said, trying to channel Amy. And then, thinking of Joy, I added, "Maybe this will turn out to be good for Ray and Roxie."

"Good, how? You mean they go bankrupt and discover that they were never meant to run the Breeze? That instead they should be organic sheep herders?"

I winced. "All right, I agree: this is bad."

"It's a disaster. Did you see his discount on craft beers? He's deliberately targeting beer drinkers." Scottie frowned and then mumbled, "And still, he won't carry Sugar Glider."

I glanced at him. His frown looked so familiar. Like the way he'd frowned when he was 5 years old when he didn't get the computer he wanted for his birthday. Or at age 7, when Mom and Dad wouldn't let him use the money he'd earned selling lost-and-found items on eBay to buy a dirt bike. I couldn't help but smile. Usually, Scottie's frown hardened into a stubborn determination to win. If Scottie's past was any indication, he'd soon convince all of Allington to buy, sell, and drink Sugar Glider. God help us.

"Come on," I said. "I want to talk to Lester. Maybe you can change his mind about Sugar Glider. It's worth another try."

He smiled. "You're right, Park. It's always worth another try."

Inside the wine bar, servers rushed from the counter to the tables, bringing food and drinks to customers. I recognized lots of people. And tried hard not to judge them for coming to Lester's. Once the Breeze reopened, they'd be back again.

At least I hoped so.

Lester stood behind the bar. He wasn't serving people. Instead, he watched as a bartender did the work. Must be a new hire. His staff was already growing.

With his arms crossed over his chest, he had a satisfied smile on his face. If he was a cartoon with a caption, the text would read: "To Lester Huxley, everything was going according to plan."

Calm down, Park. He was happy about his business doing well. That didn't constitute suspicious behavior, did it?

"Hi, Lester," I said, slipping into a narrow space between two customers.

He frowned. "Miss Lee. Would you like to order a drink?"

"I'm here on *Gazette* business. I was hoping to ask you some questions about your brother."

The man next to me glanced at me, and then, clearly curious, at Lester.

Lester's frown deepened. He nodded toward a door in the back.

"Come into my office," he said.

I followed him into the office and Scottie tagged along.

"You don't work at *The Gazette*, do you?" Lester said.

Scottie shrugged. "I'm Park's wingman."

Lester hesitated, no doubt realizing that Scottie had a pitch ready for him. But he relented and closed the door behind us.

His office was small and cramped. Just enough room for a desk, some filing cabinets, and four chairs. His was the biggest, most comfortable. Ours were the modern office equivalent of Shaker chairs. Hard.

As he sank down into his chair, I spotted something on the tabletop: next to a framed photograph of a man in a military uniform lay a leather-bound Bible. It made me think of the card from Concordia House, the one with the prayer. He must've seen me staring at the Bible, because he grabbed it, opened a drawer, and put it away. As if it were something private.

"My condolences," I began, getting out my notebook and flipping it open to a blank page. "I'm sorry to come with questions during your time of grief, and I understand if—"

"Save the hokey stuff," Lester said, cutting me off. "I

didn't have anything to do with my lowlife brother. We cut ties many years ago."

"But his death—"

"—was regrettable. Tragic, even, because obviously he'd made some attempt to straighten himself out. And he failed."

"So you knew he was at Concordia House."

Lester shrugged. "I heard things through the grapevine. People would tell me things. He was still my little—" He paused, put a fist to his mouth, and coughed. Something caught in his throat. "—my brother." He went on, quickly, "So, what exactly do you want to know?"

"Did the two of you talk?"

"Not really."

"Not really?"

"That's what I said. Not really. Next question."

I wanted to challenge him. *Not really*, I jotted down in my notebook. And, *What isn't he telling me?*

"What can you tell me about Iggy? What was he like?"

"He was a drunk," Lester said.

"Apart from his addiction," I said, trying to keep my voice steady. Lester's callousness was hard to stomach. "What was he like as a kid?"

"Unambitious in school. Always taking short cuts. Never putting in a full day of hard work. And if you can't do that—"

"Then you can't do anything," Scottie said.

I glanced at him, a gentle warning. Lester eyed Scottie, too, with a frown.

But Scottie ignored the warnings. "Lester, you're the kind of guy who builds things. I get that. So where did you get your inspiration from? I mean, someone must've pushed you to be a success."

Lester turned the framed photograph of the man in uniform, angling it toward us. "My dad. Lester Senior."

"A man of action," Scottie said, nodding with approval.

"You'd better believe it. He saw action in Vietnam and the Persian Gulf during Operation Desert Storm. He liked to say, 'If a man is big enough, every challenge becomes small.'"

"And he passed that on to his sons."

"Well—" Lester turned the picture of his dad toward him. Then looked at us again. "—at least he passed it on to one of his sons."

Scottie nodded. "It was a gift."

"A darn big one, yeah."

"Strange that your brother didn't appreciate it."

Lester harrumphed. "*Strange* isn't the right word. Mom coddled him. Dad always said so. If Dad hadn't been away so much, he'd have whipped some sense into Iggy. But by the time Dad retired from the Army, it was too late. Iggy was already a mess."

"Where's your mom now?"

"Oh, she's passed. They all have." Lester glanced away, something passing over his face. Like a shadow. His voice dropped a notch. "They're all gone now."

Was it my imagination, or did his shoulders slump a little?

If they did, he quickly straightened up and stared at us with his usual hard gaze.

"I don't have more time to waste," he said, getting up from his chair. "I've got to get back to work."

I thanked him for his time. So did Scottie.

At the door, Lester put a hand on Scottie's shoulder.

"I feel we see eye-to-eye, young man. That beer of yours, Sugar Slider—"

"Sugar Glider."

"Right. Let's talk about that sometime soon."

Scottie turned and gave Lester his hand, and the two of them shook. A real manly handshake. I expected them both to growl at each other like bears.

The whole thing was ridiculous—and also brilliant.

Outside the wine bar, I gave Scottie a nudge. "You sneaky rat. You totally manipulated him." I laughed. "I never saw you as the psychological kind."

Scottie shrugged. "I'm not. But I read a lot of entrepreneur memoirs, and the big tycoons almost all have daddy issues. My regret is sometimes that Dad is just so darn nice. If he'd been a jerk, imagine what I could've accomplished by now. Anyway, I saw the framed photograph, and it gave me an idea..."

I put an arm around Scottie. "It was pure genius."

"It was, wasn't it?" Scottie beamed. "And now I may have a new Sugar Glider customer, too."

15

Lee family dinners usually happened at Broadstairs House, the big old Victorian I lived in with Mom, Dad, Scottie, and Joy. But tonight we were descending on Roxie and Ray's place. A white farmhouse-style house with a wraparound porch.

I walked in the front door, and I heard a thrumming of paws on the carpeting inside and then Wimsey launched himself at me. His paws hit my stomach, and I fell backward, hitting the door behind me. Thankfully, it was closed, or I would've gone tumbling down the front steps.

Wimsey barked happily.

"Hey, Wimsey," I said, rubbing him in all the places he loved. "Good to see you, too."

Roxie came and gently pulled Wimsey off me.

"Thanks for coming, Park. With the Breeze closed, we're desperate for company."

"But you always say the two of you don't have enough time together," I said.

"I know," Roxie said with a laugh. "But then the house feels so empty."

"I'll move in with you, if you want," I said.

We hugged. She took a step back, but kept hold of my arms. A big smile on her face. "You're welcome to move in any time."

I followed her inside and Wimsey padded along with us. What would it be like to live with Ray, Roxie, and Wimsey? On the walls, artwork hung askew. I stepped on a squishy dog toy that let out a squeak. Then maneuvered around a pile of boxes to get through the doorway to the kitchen.

As always at our family gatherings, everyone had piled into the kitchen.

Ray was moving back and forth at the stove, looking harried as he stirred and covered and uncovered pots. A pile of dirty dishes had been exiled to the sink. Dad was leaning against the counter, a glass of wine in hand as he talked to Ray.

Joy, Amy, and Mom stood around the kitchen table, chopping vegetables and tossing them into a giant salad bowl. Scottie was rummaging in the fridge, the door wide open. In his hand, he held a six-pack of Sugar Glider beers.

"It's impossible to find space," he complained. "Where can I put my beers?"

"Take out that Tupperware," Roxie suggested, reaching over his shoulder to grab the container. "And this one, too." She held the containers up to the light and winced. "It's moldy, anyway."

Everything at the Breeze was clean and tidy. Inventory labeled and tracked. Nothing ever past its best before date. No tasks left undone for tomorrow. But Roxie and Ray's own home must be where they allowed their chaos to reign—it was a receptacle for dog toys, half-empty containers of store-bought guacamole (which they'd never serve at the Breeze —only freshly made guac would do), old copies of *The*

Allington Gazette (partly ripped by eager paws), dirty clothes and dirty dishes, and piles of papers that probably, hopefully didn't hide long overdue electricity bills.

Did I want to move in with Ray, Roxie, and Wimsey? No. Despite Scottie and Joy occasionally driving me crazy (well, mostly Scottie), my life at Broadstairs House was pretty close to perfect. And maybe Amy and Mom weren't the only Lee family members with a touch of OCD. The mess here was just beyond my own tipping point.

I joined Ray at the stove. "Hey, brother. Put me to work."

Ray let out a sigh of relief. "Finally, backup arrives."

He put me in charge of the pasta while he focused on the sauce.

Soon, we had things under control.

"So, how're you doing?"

Ray shrugged. "The county coroner and forensics have been working overtime. Mom says we should get the green light to reopen soon."

"And have they found anything?"

Behind me, Mom said, "That's confidential. I can't discuss ongoing cases."

I turned to her. "Since when?"

"Well, since the murder happened at Ray and Roxie's business. This could look like a serious conflict of interest."

Ray and I exchanged glances, and we couldn't help but smile. Mom's idea of police protocol was strict, except when it came to family. Then it became fluid. Dinner conversation at Broadstairs House often included blow-by-blows of traffic violations, not to mention detailed summaries of forensics reports. "Confidential" was a word that didn't apply to my family.

I said, "Mom, any indication this might go back to Lester Huxley?"

Mom sighed, easily giving up any attempt to keep the investigation under wraps. "Oh, all right. Of course we're looking at Lester. Why? What've you learned?"

"Actually, I was the one who learned something," Scottie said and took a swig of Sugar Glider. He made a satisfied "aaah" sound and admired the label on the bottle. As if he were modeling for an ad.

Mom raised an eyebrow. "Oh?"

I told her—and everyone else listening—about our visit to Lester's wine bar a couple of hours ago. How callous Lester had seemed about Iggy. But also how he'd appeared to be keeping a lid on his emotions.

"He clearly admires his dad," I said.

"Hero worship," Dad said. "Though I don't know that Lester Sr. deserved the worship."

I turned to Dad. "Why not?"

"Lester Sr. was a hard man. And if rumors are true, he treated his wife and kids with the tenderness of a drill sergeant."

"The rumors about Lester Sr.," Mom said, shaking her head, "are unfortunately true. His idea of parenting was all about discipline. Not that boundaries aren't good. Or rules. You know kids, they—"

"—thrive on predictability," Amy, Joy, Scottie, Ray, and I said in unison. We kids had heard Mom say that so many times.

Mom made her not-impressed face and added, "Lester Sr. wasn't above using the belt to enforce his ideas of right and wrong."

Dad said, "And I suspect Lester Jr. embraced his dad's philosophy. Competition, discipline, hard-heartedness. But Iggy didn't."

"Or he couldn't," Mom added. "He needed something

different. Something his dad despised. I remember that when Lester Sr. was still alive, he treated Iggy with such disdain. It was hard to watch. Eventually, he publicly disowned his youngest son."

"I guess Lester Jr. took a page out of his old man's book," I said. "The way he talked about Iggy sounded like he despised and dismissed him. I guess Iggy didn't live up to Lester's ideas of success. It must've been hard for Iggy—to see his brother succeed, while he himself struggled."

"Well, success is all in the eye of the beholder," Dad said.

"Meaning what?"

"Meaning that Lester's wine bar is just his latest attempt at success."

"He's failed a lot?"

Dad nodded. "More than most, maybe."

"Didn't he used to run Fab4Fitness?" Joy asked.

"That's right," Scottie said. "Along with three business partners. But Lester pulled out. 'Irreconcilable differences.' Rumor is Lester is difficult to work with."

I wasn't surprised Scottie knew this bit of gossip. He didn't pay attention to Allington's grapevine when it came to interpersonal squabbles—unless, of course, it was about entrepreneurs. His kind of people. His kind of squabbles.

We moved into the dining room and enjoyed a delicious dinner—Ray had made his famous spaghetti bolognese. We sat for hours, talking. The topic shifted from the crime investigation to Amy's congregation, Joy's latest maternity yoga class, and on to Scottie's ambitions for Sugar Glider.

We spoke over each other, eager to share our stories, competing with each other and with the music on the speakers. We laughed. We even tolerated Mom and Dad singing along to old songs from their youth.

And occasionally, someone got the task of taking

Wimsey out into the backyard or down to the basement to play with him. If he didn't get regular playtime, he'd end up chewing something to a pulp.

I spent some time in the finished basement playing with him. The muffled sound of voices and music came through the floor. Wimsey had a bed down here. But it wasn't just a dog cave—it was also a man cave with a pool table, an exercise bike, and a fully stocked bar. A place for Ray to practice his bartending skills.

Ray appeared at the bottom of the stairs. I hadn't heard him approach.

"Come up again," he said. "Wimsey can relax a little. Right, Wimsey?"

Wimsey barked and went flying toward Ray, showing no signs of wanting to relax. Ray laughed and scratched him behind his ears.

Upstairs, things were winding down. It had been a classic Lee family evening, and for much of the time, we hadn't talked about burglaries or murders. It had been a nice respite from the bad news at the Breeze.

But after saying goodnight to Roxie, Ray, and Wimsey, I turned down the ride back to Broadstairs House with Mom, Dad, Scottie, and Joy. I wanted to walk. I needed the time to think.

My mind circled the same handful of clues I'd already circled a hundred times now. Iggy breaking into the Breeze and sabotaging the fermentation tanks. The card from Concordia House outside Lester's wine bar. Iggy's call to *The Gazette*. His bloody body at the Breeze.

As I sauntered down Main Street, thinking through the details again, I glanced at a lamppost. Then stopped and doubled back.

I recognized the poster plastered to the lamppost. It

advertised the Breeze, and was part of Roxie's marketing campaign. The poster showed an illustration of Ray and Roxie in the foreground with the Breeze behind them, plus giant letters promising "Great Food" and "Great Beer" and "Great Memories."

But someone had ripped the poster. Torn two-thirds of it off, so all that remained was the word "Great" and part of Ray's face.

I walked on. At the next lamppost, the poster had been ripped, too. And at the next lamp post as well. In fact, all along Main Street, the Breeze's posters had been vandalized.

Who would do such a thing?

Then I spotted a poster in the window of a convenience store. Its bright, bold colors demanded my attention. Its big letters called out: "Lakeview Wine Bar: The best food and drink on the Allington docks!"

Lester.

Was this all about Lester wanting customers at all costs? And envying Ray and Roxie's success? If so, he must be willing to go far to win—so far, in fact, that he'd sabotage the Breeze.

Given his dad's philosophy—*competition, discipline, hard-heartedness*—that might make sense. But it was one thing to rip up posters. And quite another to murder your own brother.

16

Early the next morning, I stepped into Fab4Fitness.

The place was all mirrors, white walls, and shiny workout machines. Thumping electronic music played over speakers and competed with another rhythm: the pounding of sneakers on conveyor belts. Near the back, the discs on barbells clicked together.

Even this early, the place was half full of people. Some looking groggy with sleep. But just as many looking focused. Sweat already blooming on their shirts.

I recognized several people. Sandra and Dani were lifting weights. Dumbbells.

Near them, Johnny Boudreau was lying on his back, pushing up a barbell so loaded with discs, I expected him to be crushed under the weight. But he lifted it, the muscles in his body standing out. His biceps rippled, making the tattoo on his left arm move—the heart with D and "grandma" dancing.

And then there was Wally Wareham. He was on an elliptical. Legs and arms swinging back and forth. Looking exhausted, with bags under his eyes.

And only a couple of machines away from him—I sighed—Ray moved on an elliptical, too. Did Wally follow Ray around town? Scottie spent hours watching videos online—and listening to podcasts—where entrepreneurs detailed the daily routines that underpinned their success. Was that why Wally was here—trying to emulate Ray's success?

A metal staircase—as simple and solid as the one at the Breeze leading to the fermentation tanks—rose to a door that said "Office." I climbed above the thumping workouts and knocked on the door.

"Come in," a voice hollered from inside.

The office was long and rectangular, with ample space for the four desks. Only one of them appeared to be occupied. The other three stood empty, their surfaces clear of any items.

Once I closed the door behind me, the gym sounds became muffled and distant. It was a relief.

A lean, athletic man got up from his desk. Short haircut. A smile that belonged in an ad for gum or toothpaste. He stepped toward me, hand outstretched.

We shook.

"Ravi," he said.

I explained my errand—that I was a reporter at *The Gazette* and that I was writing a profile on Iggy Huxley.

"Then I know exactly why you came to me," Ravi said, his brown eyes twinkling with amusement. "Lester."

I nodded.

Ravi stepped over to the bank of windows overlooking the gym.

He gestured for me to look. "See all this? When we started off, the gym was half the size and looked like Rocky's first gym. Concrete. A few simple machines and weights.

Barebones. And now it's the coolest fitness center in Allington."

"When you say 'we'..."

"I mean Lester, too. And Mark and Jesse. All four of us."

A realization flashed in my mind, a tiny fireworks explosion. "Fab4Fitness. I never realized before..."

"No, no one does. It's a silly name. But at least now that I'm the only one of the Fab 4 left, people don't think the name is about its founders. It's about feeling fabulous about fitness." He smiled. "Anyway, Mark was the first to leave. His wife got a big-time job out in Silicon Valley, so they moved to California. The rest of us bought him out. No hard feelings. Then Jesse died in a skiing accident..."

He slowly shook his head.

"I'm sorry," I said.

"It's a long time ago," he said. "But I guess I'll always feel it." He touched his chest right about where his heart would be. "Anyway, how much do you want to know about the business and Lester?"

"Everything," I said. "If you feel comfortable sharing."

"None of this is secret. And it's nothing I wouldn't tell my neighbors." He sucked in a breath of air and let it out. "For a while after Jesse died, I considered shutting the business. It didn't feel right without him. But Lester was dead set against it. He told me to move on." Ravi winced. "Lester can be so callous. Cold as stone. But in his own way, inadvertently, he helped me during my grief. He and I had more than enough work to keep us busy. It kept me moving forward. Which I needed."

He paused. I sensed a "But then..." coming.

"But then," Ravi said with a sigh, "Lester started showing his true colors. I guess Jesse and Mark and I had naturally hampered Lester's less savory ambitions. But with just the two of us, it was harder for me to control."

"Control what?"

"Lester believed in 'easy money.' That's what he called it himself. Deals that looked good but actually weren't. Hidden fees. Increasing revenue by locking customers into unfair contracts. In my view, if we made the gym a success for our customers, it'd be a success for us, and I assumed Lester shared that vision. I was wrong. It nearly cost me the business."

"People weren't happy?"

"The complaints poured in. Customers left in droves—and they left angry. It took a lot of work to undo that damage." He shrugged. "Long story short, I confronted Lester and gave him a choice: the nasty business mindset goes or I go. Lester chose a third way."

"He left."

Ravi nodded. "He demanded I buy him out and named a ridiculous price. I would've paid above market value, but what he wanted was so absurd, I couldn't possibly honor it. In the end, lawyers got involved. Lester left with half of what he'd asked for. He left convinced that I had wronged him."

"You're not friends anymore?"

"No. And honestly, I wonder whether it's possible for Lester to remain friends with anyone."

"What about his family?" I asked. "Did he ever talk about his brother?"

"No, Lester never shared anything personal."

I thanked Ravi for his time. We shook hands, and he said, "Any time."

As he opened the door for me, he said, "I just remembered. Lester didn't talk about his family, as such. But sometimes he'd regurgitate these maxims he'd learned from his dad. He kept a framed photograph of his dad on his desk. Military guy. And judging by the maxims, he was tough. Lester used to say stuff like 'a commander who cannot develop proper discipline must be replaced.' And 'discipline is the soul of an army.' As if this was a military operation, not a fitness center. I can't imagine how that thinking will serve him well in running a wine bar." He shook his head. "But then, Lester's always been a hopeless entrepreneur. The worst kind. He believes he's got the Midas touch, but it's actually the opposite: whatever he touches turns to rot."

His wording sent a little shockwave through me. It reminded me of Amy's sermon and the quote from Proverbs: *A heart at peace gives life to the body, but envy rots the bones.*

17

The door shut behind me. For a moment, I paused on the landing at the top of the metal staircase. One hand on the railing. It was almost a relief to hear Ravi's description of Lester. Somehow, it suggested, this all came back to Iggy and Lester.

This murder really had nothing to do with the Breeze. And why would it? The Breeze was an oasis—a place where people felt good. It wasn't just a part of my family. It was its own little family.

Heading down the staircase, I thought of the many birthday parties or impromptu Friday night drinks I'd enjoyed at the Breeze over the years, and it put a smile on my face.

As I came closer to the bottom, I caught sight of Ray and Sandra chatting below.

"Just swapping horror stories from bartending school," Ray told me.

"There was this cocktail we had to make for the exam," Sandra said.

"The Ramos Gin Fiz."

"Yes!"

Ray shook his head, a rueful smile on his face. "It's why I failed my final exam and had to redo it. Even then, it was pure luck I got it right the next time. I've never cracked the code on the Ramos Gin Fiz."

"I can show you the trick to getting the foaminess just right."

"I'd love that."

I joined them. Listening to them talk about bartending was like listening to Scottie talk about business, Joy about yoga, or Dad about the intricacies of typewriter mechanics. I didn't understand half of it, but I could appreciate the pleasure they obviously got from the conversation. It was the pleasure that friends get from geeking out about their shared passions.

I couldn't help but smile.

Dani joined us. "Ready to head back, shower, and then grab breakfast?" she asked Sandra. Sandra nodded. She turned to me and said, "I don't have a car, so I'm dependent on Dani."

"*Dependent* makes it sound like I'm your mom," Dani said and laughed.

The door to the gym opened and Roxie came striding toward us. Even at a distance, I could tell she was excited about something.

"Yay, it's a Breeze reunion," Dani said with a smile.

"And I've got good news," Roxie said.

"Is it true?" Ray put a sweaty hand on my arm and gripped it. Clearly excited. "Did Mom give the green light? Can we reopen?"

Roxie, grinning, nodded, and Ray let go of me and threw his arms around her, lifting her off the ground as she laughed.

"Put me down, you sweaty beast."

I glanced over at Dani and Sandra. Dani was grinning even more. But Sandra's mood seemed to have shifted. She looked downcast. With her arms across her chest, she hugged herself.

Dani noticed, too, and nudged her friend. "Hey, what happened? You all right?"

"Guess I'm just nervous about starting work."

Dani studied her. Then glanced at Ray and Roxie, who were leaning close together, speaking intimately. No doubt about the future of the Breeze. Roxie touched Ray's face, placing a hand on his cheek. Lovingly.

Dani added quietly, "And maybe this is about Joe, too? About missing him?"

Sandra shrugged and looked down at her feet.

It made sense. Sandra must be missing her fiancé. And did some small part of her still feel something for Ray? If nothing else, Ray and Roxie's love-birding must be a reminder of what Sandra was waiting for.

I took a step closer to Sandra and Dani.

"I heard about your fiancé," I said. "You must be excited to see him again."

Sandra smiled. A sad smile. "You can't imagine. And most days, I'm fine with it. I know it's just a matter of time. But other times..."

"The waiting is hard," I said.

She nodded. "So hard." She frowned. "But I've waited this long for us to be reunited. And every day, I get closer. One step closer to the rest of my life." She sighed and straightened up. Then brightened. A smile spread across her face. "But there's no point in wallowing in self-pity. The Breeze is opening again, and I've got work to do."

Dani laughed. "Sandra, you're the sunniest person I know."

I remembered Sandra's goth style years ago. Not what you'd describe as sunny. But she'd been the one to lift Ray out of his dark period. Which just proved that you couldn't judge a book by its cover.

Dani turned back to Roxie and Ray. "So, guys. When do we reopen?"

"Technically, we can open right away," Roxie said. "But we need to clean and get a new batch of beer ready. So, tomorrow we welcome the customers back again." She nudged me. "Hey, want to join us for our staff meeting today?"

"Uh, sure. But why would you want me there—won't I be a distraction?"

"Not if you come on behalf of *The Gazette*." She grinned. "Maybe snap a few photos. We could use a front-page mention about the reopening."

"Oh." I realized what she was asking. Then smiled. "You got it."

Wally joined us, mopping sweat off his face. "Hey, guys. Did I hear right? You're reopening?" He grinned. "That's awesome news. I can't wait to hang out at the Breeze again."

Roxie looked at Ray. It was a quick glance that probably only I noticed. But it reminded me of what Roxie thought of Wally. She didn't like how he clung to Ray.

Johnny, apparently also done with his workout, came lumbering past us. Dani had been right—this was a big Breeze reunion.

"Hey, Johnny," Ray said with a big smile. "Did you hear? The Breeze is reopening."

Johnny frowned. He glanced at Wally—who smiled, gave a little nod in place of a goodbye, and headed back to the exercise machines—and then Johnny looked back at Ray with an expression I couldn't parse. Confusion? Resentment? Maybe both?

"Guess you'll want me to work overtime again," he grumbled.

"Johnny—" Roxie said, her voice sharp, but Ray put a hand on her arm, stopping her. He gave her a little shake of the head.

Johnny trudged past us. I watched him go, his massive shoulders slumped. His head drawn into himself like an angry turtle. A snapping turtle.

"We'll stick to our normal time for the staff meeting, Johnny," Ray called after him, obviously trying to keep the irritation out of his voice. "See you there."

Ray and Roxie exchanged glances. Both displeased. Dani watched them closely, lips pressed together. She said, "Here we go again. He's going to mess things up for the rest of us. Again and again and again."

"It'll work it out," Ray said.

"Like it's worked out so far?" Dani snapped. Then turned to Sandra. "Come on, let's go."

Dani strode past Ray and Roxie. Sandra gave them a little smile and wave as she hurried after her friend. The door closed behind them.

Something about Dani's intensity made me wonder. Was it just workplace drama between her and Johnny, or did she resent him for some other reason? Not that she needed another reason. Johnny didn't do himself any favors. He was easy to dislike.

Ray took a deep breath and let out a sigh. He rubbed the back of his neck. "Why do I feel like I've made a mess of things?"

"Because you have," Roxie said, frowning. "You should've listened to me and fired Johnny ages ago."

"Oh, come on," Ray said. "We agreed that—"

"No. You agreed with yourself to give him another chance."

"And if we fired everyone who made a mistake, then—"

"That's not what I said!"

I crept past them and eased the door open. Quietly escaping the quarrel. So much for my idea about the Breeze being one big happy family.

18

Later that day at the Breeze staff meeting, we gathered at the bar. About ten of us. Me. Ray. Roxie. Dani. The kitchen staff. Plus a team of servers—some were regulars, others freelancers who stepped in during high season or to cover for others.

Sandra came rushing in at the last minute, apologizing for her "tardiness."

"My boyfriend called," she said. "With the time difference, it's hard to catch each other."

"Don't worry—you're on time," Roxie said, and then looked around, apparently taking a silent roll call.

I leaned against the bar next to the chef and one of the other servers. Everyone had turned up on time. Except Johnny. He hadn't shown.

"Big surprise," Dani muttered.

Roxie checked her watch and said, "We'll get started and hopefully Johnny will join us soon."

Ray clapped his hands together. "All right. First, it's worth celebrating that we're back in business."

Everyone applauded. Ray grinned and held up a hand for quiet.

"But we've got a lot of work to do. A lot of catching up. When those doors open, we won't have enough of our own beer on tap to meet demand. We'll be dropping prices on bottled beers to make up for it."

If Scottie heard that, he'd be trying to convince Ray to buy more Sugar Glider. Well, I wouldn't be the one to tell Scottie—let Ray deal with that.

Ray detailed what food and drink needed to be restocked. Then moved on to cleaning. "That's the first order of business. We need to give the entire brewery, bar, and restaurant a deep clean."

The door opened and Johnny plodded inside.

"Hey, Johnny," Ray said. "I was just explaining what we need to clean."

Johnny frowned. "Fine," he grumbled.

Ray added, "After what happened in the brewery, I want you to do a deep, deep clean."

Johnny muttered something. I couldn't make it out. One word stood out, though: "vermin."

Ray frowned, apparently not hearing all of it either.

But Dani did. "Johnny," she snapped. "That's uncool. Iggy was a person. A person struggling with addiction. And actually he could be a sweet guy."

Johnny snorted. "As if you knew him."

"Of course I did. I knew him from Concordia House. Sandra and I volunteer there."

"That's right." Sandra stepped up to her friend's side and put a hand on her arm. "At Concordia, we learn how to help people in trouble." She glanced at Dani. "And we learn something else, too—how not to escalate a confrontation. Remember, Dani?"

Dani let out a long breath. "Yeah, I remember," she mumbled, obviously mollified by her friend's comment about not escalating a conflict.

This was a smooth move by Sandra. She'd shown her support for her friend while also de-escalating the situation.

Roxie apparently thought so, too. She nodded at Sandra and mouthed the words "thank you."

But Sandra's attention was back on Ray.

Ray sighed. "Johnny, whatever's bothering you, why don't you leave it at the door? We can talk it over later. Right now, we all need to work together to get the Breeze ready. And let's put on some good music—no reason we can't have fun while scrubbing this place."

Johnny's frown didn't vanish. But he kept his mouth shut —a thin, resentful line—as Ray continued to outline the tasks and who would do what.

Meanwhile, Roxie gave me some details for *The Gazette* article on special deals they'd be running at the Breeze. But I kept glancing over at Johnny, studying that frown on his face. The guy had a serious chip on his shoulder. Occasionally, he'd glance at Dani and his frown would deepen. And Dani, who was usually so happy and nice to everyone, scowled back at him.

She'd clearly been upset by what he said about Iggy.

Because she knew him from Concordia House. And so did Sandra.

It was time I took a closer look at Concordia.

19

Concordia House wasn't a house. It was located in a red-brick office building that had seen better days. Inside, though, the reception area was clean, bright, and cheerful, despite an old linoleum floor and couches whose stuffing had sunk into their recesses, leaving deep indentations. "Comfortably worn" might be a nice way to put it. A few potted plants brightened up the place, and there was a stack of magazines and books to entertain people as they waited.

A statue of Jesus in flowing robes stood on a pedestal overlooking the reception area.

A wide arched doorway led down a corridor to a cafeteria. I could just make out rows of tables on a white-tiled floor. Closer to me was a stairwell with steps going up as well as down. Assuming Iggy had lived at Concordia for a while, his room would be somewhere up there.

On the wall near a coffee machine hung a poster with the recovery center's mission: "We provide humane services and guidance to individuals affected by substance use, giving them the serenity, courage, and wisdom for lifelong recovery."

That phrase, "serenity, courage, and wisdom" must be a nod to the Serenity Prayer.

Next to the poster was a corkboard. Pins held polaroids of staff in place, a little label underneath each, indicating the name and their position. Most were marked "volunteer."

"Parker," a voice said behind me, and I turned.

Mona Macintosh was striding toward me, a smile on her face.

I thanked her for seeing me.

"Anything for a Lee family member," she said. "Your family's done a lot for us here at Concordia."

"Oh?"

"Sure. Your mom's always a big help, and so empathetic toward our clients. And Amy's contributions and ministering are important sources of nourishment for our people." She paused. "And then there's Ray, of course." Something flickered in her eyes when she said Ray's name. Her smile shifted. "Ray's always been generous in donating food and soft drinks."

"So the Breeze has done a lot for Concordia House," I said, wondering what Mona wasn't telling me about Ray. A thought occurred to me. "But it's not the only business involved, is it?"

"Oh, we're lucky to get support from many."

"That new wine bar, maybe?"

"Wine bar?" She shook her head. "But Zephyr Bar supports us."

"Wally's bar?"

"That's right. He donates surplus drinks and food. He drops by at least once a week."

I frowned. Wally again.

Mona continued: "We rely a lot on donations. Not to mention volunteers."

I gestured toward the corkboard. "Yeah, I saw several familiar faces. Like Dani and Sandra."

"They're fairly recent joiners. We also have folks who've been volunteering since the day we opened."

"Do they come here a lot—Dani and Sandra?"

"Two-three times a week."

"And did they know Iggy Huxley well?"

Mona frowned. She pressed her lips together. Then gave me an emphatic shake of the head. A clear no.

"I can't discuss clients. Past or present."

"Fair enough," I said. "But if he stayed here, I would love to see his room. It would give me an insight into what his life was like at Concordia. For the article I'm writing."

And for my own nosiness. Iggy might've had personal items that could point to what motivated him to break into the Breeze.

But Mona shook her head again. "We respect residents' privacy. It's hugely important. This is a sanctuary for them. A safe space. I can't compromise on that." She smiled again. "But I'm very happy to tell you more about our work at Concordia House."

So we settled down in the sagging sofa with cups of strong coffee, and I learned all about Concordia House's mission, vision, and history. Without a single reference to Iggy Huxley.

I nodded. I jotted down notes. Stuff I could've read on Concordia's website. Now and then, when Mona wasn't paying attention, I'd glance over at the staircase. If only I could sneak up those stairs and look around Iggy's room...

"I could be wrong," I said as Joy reached over with the water jug to serve me. "But I got the strange feeling that Mona Macintosh was hiding something from me. Something about Ray."

Scottie laughed. "Obviously."

"What do you mean, *obviously*?"

"You don't remember?" Scottie grinned across the dinner table at me. "Crazy Mona. That's what we called her when she dated Ray."

"Scottie," Mom said, berating him. She'd finished her baked salmon and was focusing on her salad. Dad, having served himself the last piece of salmon, heaped mustard onto his plate. We were sitting at the kitchen table, eating a late dinner. Outside Broadstairs House, night had fallen.

"What, Mom?" Scottie said. "Didn't we call her that?"

"The past is past, and so we can let it go," Joy said. She spoke like a guru. A gently guiding voice of kindness. "Mona is a different person now."

"Wait," I said. "Back up. Why did you call her Crazy Mona?"

"You really don't remember?" Scottie laughed, apparently equally unfazed by Mom's lecturing tone as by Joy's gentle guidance. "Ray dated her for a while. Before his dark and brooding period, he went through a phase where every relationship he touched seemed to explode into flames. And Mona definitely exploded."

"That's an exaggeration," Mom said.

"Oh, really?" Scottie gave Mom an incredulous look. "So, in your professional opinion, slashing someone's tires isn't crazy? You weren't so forgiving when it happened."

Mom frowned at a tomato on her plate, saying nothing.

"Mona slashed Ray's tires?" I asked, aware that my jaw had dropped and I was gaping at Scottie.

He smiled and leaned back in his chair, obviously enjoying the attention.

"Yeah, and Ray was visiting his new girlfriend at the time."

"New girlfriend?"

Scottie nodded. "After dumping Mona. And this one lived at the top of Chestnut Hill. So Ray comes out, all swagger, and doesn't notice the tires are slashed. Gets in. Puts the car in drive and—" Scottie laughed. "It was a miracle he didn't crash."

"How could he be sure it was Mona?"

"Well, he suspected it was one of his ex-girlfriends."

Scottie glanced at Mom. Mom's interest in her salad deepened.

"If she didn't tell him, then how—?" I stopped myself, suddenly realizing. "Oh, I see. Mom—you ran the prints and got a match."

"Except she didn't have a prior conviction," Scottie said, a smug smile on his face. Sometimes he seemed distracted during weeknight dinners. Not this time. He was thoroughly enjoying himself. "So, if her fingerprints weren't on file, how did Mom find out?"

"Mom," I said. I tried to meet her eye. But she kept pecking at her salad. "If you didn't have Mona's prints on file, then you'd need to get them somehow. And that's against regulations." I thought about it some more. I frowned. "Hey, but if you didn't know it was Mona, then—" I put a hand to my mouth, shocked. "No."

Mom looked up. "I did what I did. I'm not proud of it."

Dad chuckled, leaning closer to Mom and putting an arm around her back and giving her a squeeze. "The past is past. Right, Joy?"

"Right," Joy said, smiling.

I leaned forward in my seat. "You lifted the fingerprints of all of Ray's ex-girlfriends so you could find the culprit."

Mom winced. "I told you, I'm not proud of it." Then her voice dropped to a mumble. "But in the end, I got the perp."

Everyone burst out laughing—Scottie, Dad, me, even Joy couldn't contain her laughter—and for a split second, Mom glared at us. Then the frown eased off her face, and she smiled, too.

"I guess sometimes Mama Bear can't resist," she said.

"So, Mama Bear," I said, still laughing. "Did you throw Crazy Mona in the slammer?"

Mom shook her head. "No, I threatened to. But instead I convinced Ray to have a civilized conversation with her."

"A confrontation? Ray must've loved that."

"Oh, Ray did what he needed to do. And Mona paid for the tires and backed off."

"And now Ray supports her nonprofit recovery center with donations," I said.

Mom nodded. "They're friendly now. As Joy said, the past is past."

I twirled my fork and scooped up my last piece of salmon. Chewing slowly, I gave this piece of history some thought. Once upon a time, Mona had been angry enough at Ray to slash his tires. But that was many years ago, and as Joy said, the past was the past.

Or was it?

21

Amy sat behind her desk in her office at Shepherd's Gate Church. Morning light streamed through the stained glass window behind her. In front of her on her desk sat six squat shot glasses containing a dark red liquid.

"Amy," I said as I walked in. "What in God's name are you doing?"

"Not exactly an appropriate use of our creator's name," she said with a raised eyebrow. "But I admit how strange this looks."

"Strange? It looks like you're taking shots. And it's—" I checked my watch. "—11 am."

"I'm just tasting."

I plonked down in front of her desk. "That's what they all say."

"These are six samples from different church wine suppliers. My current supplier is going out of business, so I need to switch wines."

"What's this one?" I pointed to one that had a darker hue than the others.

"Blackberry wine. Too saccharine, in my opinion. But there's one that's like a Shiraz. A hint of fruitiness without being overtly sweet."

"Jeez, you sound like Dad."

Amy smiled. "I do, don't I? Try this."

She handed me a shot glass. I took a sip. Strong, sweet flavor.

"This is more like grape soda than wine," I said. Then smiled. "I like it."

"Non-alcoholic wine made with Concord grapes."

Since it was non-alcoholic—and since it was tasty—I downed the drink and handed my sister the glass. With a raised eyebrow and an amused smile, she took the glass and moved it, along with the others, to the end of her desk. She arranged them in a neat row. She'd always had a touch of OCD.

Then she rested her arms on the tabletop and leaned forward a little, her body language showing that I had her complete attention. This was why her congregants loved her. She made you feel seen and heard.

"Tell me," she said. "What brings you here today?"

"Amy, take it easy. I'm not here to discuss a crisis of faith or anything like that. I wanted to ask you about Mona Macintosh."

Amy leaned back in her chair. "Mona? What about her?"

I explained what a hard time I was having getting information out of Mona about Iggy's stay at Concordia House. My hope was that Amy might talk to Mona and get me some intel. But Amy said she understood the importance of the recovery center's privacy policy.

"Like my own client confidentiality, it protects people who may be especially vulnerable. You understand that, don't you?"

I nodded. Sure, I understood. But still, I'd hoped Amy would help me bend the rules. I sighed. Amy never bent the rules. Not unless a higher power OK'd it.

I said, "Another thing. Last night, Scottie filled me in on the episode with Ray's slashed tires."

Amy sighed. "That was a long time ago."

"That's what Joy and Mom said. But I'm wondering if Mona might not still harbor some feelings for Ray. I mean, she was pretty obsessed with him back then. Maybe that hasn't changed."

"Mona's happily married. She left Allington for a while and met Bill Macintosh. Then brought him back here. Have you ever seen them together? If you did, you'd know that they're a pair of lovebirds. Couldn't be happier together. Whatever feelings she once had for Ray must be ancient history for her."

Then she chuckled.

"Although I do sometimes wonder whether Ray donates to Concordia House because he feels guilty about how he broke up with her. Back then, he got a new girlfriend every other month, and it seemed as if they were all obsessed with him. Mona Wareham wasn't the first or the last."

I leaned forward. "Mona *Wareham*?"

"Yeah, Wareham's her maiden name."

"You mean Mona's related to Wally Wareham, the guy who owns Zephyr Bar."

Amy nodded. "Sure. Wally is her younger brother."

She folded her hands across her stomach, leaning back in a contemplative pose. It was exactly the same pose Dad defaulted to when he was thinking.

She said, "Funny, isn't it? First Mona becomes obsessed with Ray, and now it's her baby brother's turn."

"Would you say Wally Wareham is *obsessed* with Ray?"

Amy shrugged. "How else to describe it? He follows Ray around like a puppy in love. But he's a young guy. He'll grow out of it."

I wondered about that. Mona had slashed Ray's tires because she was obsessed. How far did Wally's obsession go?

22

Zephyr Bar had only been open a couple of hours when I got there, and only a few customers graced the narrow space with the long bar. A group of guys—five of them—sat at the bar. Their faces reflecting in the mirror among the many bottles. Among them, my brother Scottie's.

"Hey, Park," he said when I slid onto the barstool next to him.

No one stood behind the bar.

"Where's Wally?"

Scottie shrugged. "On his way, I guess. I just got here."

"He and the new bartender are changing kegs in the basement," the guy next to Scottie said. I recognized him as one of Scottie's old high school buddies, DJ. Big burly guy with a beard.

"Hey, Park."

He grinned at me and took a sip of his bottled beer, looking down. Shy. I'd always suspected DJ had a crush on me, even when I was in middle school and he was in high school.

Then I recognized the bottled beer. He was drinking Sugar Glider. In fact, they all were.

"I see you're here for business," I said to Scottie, "not pleasure."

"Just sharing some beers with my buddies," he said. Then, in a low voice for my ears only, he added, "Promotion. I don't usually come to Zephyr Bar, but I heard they'd be here. These guys are regulars at several watering holes in Allington. They're perfect evangelists for my product. First, I get them hooked. Then they start asking bar owners why they don't carry Sugar Glider. Great strategy, right?"

"Uh-huh," I said, nodding. Thinking my brother was sounding like a drug dealer. But it wasn't the first time I'd heard him use this kind of language.

I leaned forward so I could talk to the others. "Hey guys. How's the beer?"

"Awesome," DJ said.

"Really nice," the guy next to him said.

The others nodded.

Wally came out of a back door, wiping his hands on the front of his shirt. "Done. Who wants to try the new IPA?"

"Me," the guys said, almost in perfect unison.

I laughed and nudged Scottie. "You'd better keep working on that strategy of yours."

Scottie frowned. I thought he was reacting to my comment. But then saw he wasn't. He was staring at something behind the bar. I followed his gaze. Not something— someone. Johnny Boudreau stood in the doorway to the back, staring at Scottie and me.

Then he mumbled something and lumbered over to Wally to help fill pint glasses.

"I'm confused," I whispered to Scottie. "Doesn't Johnny work at the Breeze anymore?"

"Last I heard, he does."

DJ leaned toward us. Apparently, our whisper wasn't as quiet as I'd thought. He said, "Johnny started a week ago. Wally's been doing pretty well and needs the extra help."

I nodded. I glanced at Johnny, who, at that moment, was looking at me. He turned away, suddenly busy with pouring the perfect pint.

So this was why he was constantly late for work. And why he was rushing out early. Zephyr Bar opened late and stayed open until dawn. If Johnny was moonlighting for Wally, he was working late into the night. With little time for sleep. No wonder he was so crabby.

As Johnny pulled a pint, he glared at the tap. His eyes flickered up. A brief glance at me. Then his focus returned to the beer.

"I wonder if Ray and Roxie know," I whispered to Scottie. Then had another thought. "Why would Wally do this? He knows Johnny works at the Breeze. If he worships Ray, like everyone seems to think, then stealing staff is a strange way to show it."

Scottie shrugged. "Maybe he's still bitter."

"Bitter?"

"Didn't you know? Wally applied for a job as a brewer at the Breeze. But Roxie and Ray turned him down."

"Oh," I said.

How might it feel, I wondered, to have your hero reject your application for a dream job? Maybe it would only make you work harder to live up to his achievements. Or maybe it would make you bitter. Resentful. Even eager for revenge.

I studied Wally. While Johnny served the guys their pints of IPA, occasionally casting wary glances my way, Wally was sitting at a laptop by the cash register, head down.

One hand resting on the back of his neck. Face pinched in a deep frown.

The laptop screen was turned away from me. But the bar's long mirror, though backed with bottle-filled shelves, caught the reflection. Giving me a peek at his screen. A small peek, but it was enough. Because the website he was studying was familiar.

It was the Breeze's website.

23

"Oh," Ray said, and ran a hand through his hair. He took a deep breath and let it out. "I suspected Johnny might be moonlighting. But at Wally's place?" He shook his head. "I never would've guessed."

It was the next morning, and we were sitting on barstools at the Breeze. Roxie was behind the counter, wiping glasses. That usually fell to Ray—or one of the other bartenders—but I got the feeling Roxie needed something to do with her hands right now. The glare she leveled at the pint glass in her hand suggested she was fighting hard not to throw it across the room. Or maybe go find Johnny or Wally and throw one of them across the room.

"Scottie told me about Wally," I said. "That you turned him down for a job at the Breeze."

Ray nodded. "I didn't think he was ready. He didn't have enough brewery experience. Roxie didn't agree."

I looked at Roxie. She shrugged. "The guy's young, but he could learn. The most important thing was that he showed enthusiasm for the work. But I'm not the master brewer. Ray would've had to teach Wally, and if Wally wasn't ready..."

"Instead, we hired someone with plenty of experience," Ray said.

"Johnny Boudreau," I said.

"Yeah. And look how that's turned out."

I wondered if Ray felt some kinship with Johnny that made all this difficult. After all, long before Ray owned the Breeze, he'd worked his fingers to the bone trying to raise enough cash for a down payment on his own place. He'd worked in a restaurant during the day, handling the brunch and lunch crowds, and then moonlighted at a bar at night. He knew all about grueling work schedules.

He sighed again. Checked his watch. "Johnny should be here any moment now. I called him this morning at his grandma's house. Got him out of bed, so we can talk."

I felt for Ray. He didn't enjoy confronting employees. Roxie was better at this stuff. But as she'd said, Ray was the master brewer, and so he had to talk to Johnny about moon-lighting for Wally.

The door to the Breeze opened, and we all looked toward it. Expecting to see Johnny.

But it was Dani who came bounding inside, a messenger bag bouncing at her hip. A big smile on her face.

"Morning, everyone," she said.

"Morning," Ray said. "You got here early again."

"I've got to transfer the beer to the conditioning tanks. Don't want to rush it. And later, we're going to do quality control."

"Quality control?" I asked.

"It means taste testing the batches."

"Tough job."

"Yup." She grinned. "But someone's gotta do it."

Dani went behind the bar to the espresso machine, made herself a cup of coffee, and then returned to our side to drink it.

The door to the Breeze opened again. This time it was Johnny. He came shuffling inside, his boots scuffing the floor. He could've auditioned for a part on *The Walking Dead*. Pale. Dark rings under his eyes. Lumbering gait. He looked terrible.

He stopped halfway to the bar. Glared at us.

"What?"

We must all have been staring at him.

Ray said, "Johnny, we need to talk. Why don't we go to the office?"

"I need a coffee first," Johnny said, approaching the bar and standing next to Ray.

Ray put a hand on Johnny's big shoulder. "Hey, buddy. I think we should meet in private."

Johnny shrugged Ray's hand off. "You can't wake a man up from a dead sleep and expect him to operate on no caffeine."

Ray and Roxie exchanged glances. She shrugged.

Johnny headed around the bar counter and stood by the espresso machine. He filled the portafilter with grounds and tamped them down. The espresso machine rumbled as the dark liquid streamed into a cup. No one spoke.

A few moments later, Johnny plonked down on a barstool with a black Americano in front of him.

He took a sip.

Ray settled down on the barstool next to him. "Johnny, I know about Zephyr Bar. I know about you working for Wally."

Johnny glanced over at me. Then back at his coffee. He shrugged. "So what? A man's got a right to work, right?"

"Actually—" Roxie began, but Ray lifted a hand, asking her to stay out of it.

She gave him a nod. Then picked up another pint glass and started wiping it furiously.

"You're right—a man does have a right to work," Ray said. "But he's got to actually do the work. All of it."

"I do the work," Johnny said.

"You do some of the work here at the Breeze. Then you do the rest at Wally's. That means that half the time you're rushing out of the Breeze without finishing your tasks. You show up late. You leave early."

"Well, you try working two jobs at the same time."

"I'm sure it's tough."

"You have no idea."

"Hold on a minute—" I said, furious that Johnny would presume Ray didn't know how hard it was. Ray, who'd worked two jobs for years to buy the Breeze. Ray, who'd scraped by on 4-5 hours of sleep day after day, who'd—

But Ray lifted a hand to me. Just as he'd done to Roxie. And it silenced me. He could handle it himself.

"Johnny," he said. "I sympathize. But it doesn't matter whether I understand your situation or not. What matters is that you've got a job to do, and you've agreed to do it—and do it well. We're a small brewery team. We depend on each other."

"Yeah," Dani said. "It's not fair that you leave extra work for me."

Ray gestured at Dani, but she didn't see his hand waving. Or else she chose to ignore it.

She went on. "Every time you rush out of the Breeze, you add an hour to my day. As if I don't have enough on my plate already."

"Don't be such a martyr," Johnny said. "You come early. You leave late. That's your choice."

"That's right. My choice. And if I choose to do extra work, that's up to me. That doesn't mean I also need to do your work for you. Just because you're too lazy to finish it."

"Lazy?" Johnny swung around on his barstool. He glowered at Dani. "Lazy?"

"Hey, I didn't mean—"

"Nobody calls me lazy." He slammed a fist down on the bar. "Nobody."

"Let's everyone calm down," Ray said, reaching out for Johnny.

But as he touched Johnny's shoulder, Johnny shoved him away. Ray went staggering back past me and slammed into Dani.

Johnny cursed and spun around. "Nobody calls me lazy."

Then he stomped out of the bar.

The door to the Breeze swung shut.

Silence. I looked at Ray. Dani was looking at him, too. But Ray was looking across the bar at Roxie.

"I screwed that up," he said.

"You did fine," she said. "Johnny's amped up. He would've exploded no matter what."

"Maybe," Ray said, not sounding convinced. I could tell he was going to blame himself for what had happened. But Johnny had been rude from the moment he walked into the bar. Ray had done his best.

Dani seemed to think so, too. She said, "Boss, Johnny's so full of thick-headed pride. He's obsessed with self-reliance. And he's convinced he's the hardest working guy in Allington."

"He's sleep deprived," Ray said, clearly trying to sympathize.

"He's full of anger," Dani said. "Sometimes I get the feeling he hates us. Really hates us. Honestly, I wouldn't put it past him to do something crazy."

"Something crazy?" I asked.

Dani shrugged. "I don't know. Like get revenge."

"You mean he'd hurt someone?"

"Oh, I don't think he'd hurt anyone," Ray said.

"Maybe not," Dani said. "But maybe he'd sabotage the Breeze."

"Dani," Ray said. "That's enough."

Dani gave me a look. I knew what that look suggested: that maybe Johnny wouldn't just consider sabotaging the Breeze—maybe he'd already done it.

24

Was Dani right? Did Johnny mastermind the sabotage at the Breeze?

I didn't buy it. If Johnny had been caught destroying one of the fermentation vats, I wouldn't be shocked. But why would he send Iggy to do his dirty work?

Still, Johnny had been lying to Roxie and Ray about moonlighting at the Zephyr Bar. Maybe he'd lied about other things, too.

I hid in the doorway to a souvenir shop. Fifty-or-so feet ahead of me, Johnny thumped toward the end of the dock. He slowed for a moment. Glanced sideways. Stopped. As if he were considering going into a store.

Only it wasn't a store.

Lester's wine bar.

"Holy moly," I muttered to myself.

What if Dani was right, and somehow Johnny was in league with Lester? That would explain how Iggy wound up in the Breeze.

Up ahead, Johnny strode away from the wine bar. For whatever reason, he'd decided not to go inside. As he rounded the corner at the end of the dock, I shot out of my hiding place and jogged after him.

I stopped at the wine bar. The door stood open. Customers sat at tables inside and outside. None of them drinking wine at this hour, of course. They were drinking coffee. And written in chalk on the specials board by the bar, it said, "Try our Julia Larke special: coffee and cake." I couldn't believe it. Now he was stealing ideas from Joy's cafe. Cafe Larke. The guy had no qualms about competition.

Lester was behind the bar, talking to a customer.

Why hadn't Johnny gone inside?

Then I saw a sheet of paper taped to the inside of the window by the entrance, and I realized how wrong I'd been. In large letters, it said, "Waiter and bartender wanted, ideally with expert knowledge of wine and beer."

Johnny hadn't been looking in at Lester. He'd stopped to look at the job ad. His time at the Breeze might be coming to an end, and he'd been tempted to apply.

So did that mean there wasn't a connection between him and Lester? Maybe not. But Dani was right—with all that anger, Johnny must be carrying around some secret resentment. The question was, what did it have to do with the Breeze? And Iggy's murder?

I hurried on, eager to catch up with Johnny. But just as I turned onto Main Street, Johnny, seated on his motorbike, roared past me. He took off, swerving around a sedan and nearly colliding with an oncoming garbage truck.

I cursed. I'd never catch up with him.

A car screeched to a halt in front of me. A police cruiser. The window lowered.

"Jump in, Park," Mom said, leaning over from the driver's side.

I yanked open the door and threw myself onto the

passenger seat. Before I could slam the door, Mom took off. Lights flashing. I pulled on my seatbelt as she swerved around cars.

I looked at her. Despite the drama of her driving, her face was calm. It took a lot to shake my mom.

"No siren?"

She shook her head. "No need to let Johnny know we're coming."

I held onto my seat as we swerved around a pickup truck, merging back into our lane just in time to avoid a collision with a delivery van. Farther ahead of us, Johnny wove in and out of traffic. But we were gaining on him.

"How come you're following Johnny?" I asked.

"Same reason you are," Mom said. "Scottie told me what the two of you discovered at Zephyr Bar. Then I heard from Ray that he'd asked Johnny to come to the Breeze this morning to talk. I figured Johnny might make a scene, so I was heading down there, just in case. On my way, I caught sight of Johnny on his motorbike. Breaking every traffic rule under the sun."

As we drove through Allington, Mom dodged cars, followed Johnny down side streets, and eventually slipped into a woodsy neighborhood on the outskirts of town. She slowed down. With only one car between us and Johnny, she hung back, careful not to look too conspicuous. Johnny had slowed, too, and now he turned up a driveway.

By the time Mom pulled the police cruiser over to the curb, Johnny was striding up a path to the front door of a house. It was a small ranch-style home with aluminum siding. A patchy lawn. Wilted flowers below heavily curtained windows.

He slipped inside and closed the door behind him.

"Time to pay a house call," Mom said, putting the car in park.

We walked up the path to the front door, and Mom rang the bell.

A little sign on the door said, "Dominique Boudreau."

"Who's Dominique Boudreau?"

"Johnny's grandma," Mom said. "More like his mom. After his parents divorced, they both left town, abandoning their little son. Dominique raised him."

Something ached in my chest—how could someone walk away from their kid like that? But before I had time to reflect more on Johnny's childhood, the door opened.

Johnny filled the entrance, a frown on his face.

"What do you want?"

"Aside from wanting to give you a speeding ticket?" Mom smiled. "I'd like to talk to you about what happened at the Breeze."

He looked over his shoulder. He stepped outside and gently closed the door.

In a low voice, almost a whisper, he said, "She's resting. The nurse is coming later today, and she'll need her strength. I don't want to wake her."

"Your grandma," Mom said. She cocked her head, studying him. "She's not well, is she?"

Johnny shook his head. Something crept into that frown of his. It wasn't anger. It was confusion and fear, and for an instant, Johnny looked like a frightened little boy. His tight t-shirt exposed his left bicep, and I caught a glimpse of his tattoo with the big heart, a D inside, and the word "grandma" above it.

"Look," he said. "I drove too fast. I shouldn't have. I don't want trouble."

"You seemed to be fine with trouble back at the Breeze," I said.

His jaw muscles flexed as he gritted his teeth. "I'm working hard. Nobody gets to call me lazy, you got it?"

"I got it." Then, as if a light bloomed in my head, I really did get it. "You're working two jobs to pay for your grandma's treatment."

He ran a hand over his brow. "Three, if you count the gardening work on the weekends, too. Truth is, Medicare doesn't cover much. She'd be better off in a nursing home where she could get around-the-clock help, but she doesn't have the money. It's not fair." His usual anger flared up again. He clenched his fists. "I guess growing old with dignity is only for the rich. Retirement homes cost an arm and a leg. So that's what I'm doing. I'm getting her an arm and a leg."

It made sense. Johnny was working unsustainable hours. Slowly killing himself. Most people wouldn't do that for themselves. But when it came to their loved ones, they'd sacrifice a lot. I thought about my own family and what I wouldn't do for them.

Mom said, "Johnny, you're doing a good thing. But you're going about it all wrong."

"Oh, yeah? And who made you the expert on my life?"

"Take it easy, big guy. All I'm suggesting is that you should talk to my son. Talk to Ray. He's got a big heart, and I bet he'd be more than willing to help you. But he can't help if you don't tell him you need help."

Johnny opened the door behind him.

For a moment, he filled the doorway, and he glared back at us.

"Grandma and I have taken care of each other forever. We don't need anyone's help."

He looked like he wanted to slam the door. But he didn't. He closed it quietly.

Mom and I stood on the doorstep, staring at each other.

"Now what?" I asked.

Mom shrugged. "If he pulls those tricks again in traffic, I won't be so lenient. But for now, let's leave this in Johnny's hands—and Ray's. I bet they can work it out."

As we headed down the path toward the police cruiser, I glanced over my shoulder. Despite Johnny's awful behavior, I felt a stab of sympathy for him. His grandma—the one person who'd stuck by his side his entire life—was dying, and he was working two jobs to give her the comfort and dignity he felt she deserved. And only barely scraping by. It would be enough to make most people bitter.

I got in Mom's car and fastened my seatbelt.

"Well?" Mom said. "Penny for your thoughts."

"I don't think Johnny sabotaged the Breeze. And I don't think he killed Iggy. He's too busy trying to make money for his grandma."

Mom nodded. "Then who did kill Iggy?"

I shook my head. "I have no idea."

25

"You thought Johnny had something to do with the sabotage?"

Ray looked at me as if I were crazy. Then took a sip of his beer as he leaned against the kitchen counter at Broadstairs House. His eyes focused on thin air. He was thinking. Finally, he shook his head.

"Nah," he said. "Not in a million years. Don't believe what Dani says—for some reason, she's really upset with Johnny. See, Johnny's the kind of guy who'll blow up. He'll lose his cool and take a swing at you. But pay someone to sneak into the brewery and ruin the batches?" He shook his head again. "It's not his style."

"And Dominique Boudreau wouldn't stand for it," Aunt Lil added. "She raised Johnny to be a decent kid. Johnny's an Aries—ruled by Mars—and he can't help his explosive nature. But he wouldn't sabotage the Breeze."

"Yeah, I already came to that conclusion," I admitted. "Besides, he's so focused on making money for his grandma, I don't think he'd risk the Breeze shutting down. He'd need to look for another job, then."

"If he keeps cutting corners at work," Scottie said from the kitchen table, "he'll need to look for another job, anyway."

"Let's hope it doesn't come to that," Amy said beside him. "Sounds like Johnny's trying to do right by his grandma."

"But he's got a job to do."

"The job is a means to an end."

"I disagree..."

As Amy and Scottie continued their argument, they shucked corn for dinner.

The Lee family dinners were a longstanding tradition. We all gathered on Sundays at Broadstairs House, where I lived with Mom, Dad, Scottie, and Joy. But this was a Thursday night. Dad had invited everyone to dinner because he'd got his hands on the first good corn of the season. Dad didn't need much of an excuse to bring us all together. Nor did the rest of us.

And somehow Aunt Lil had gotten wind of dinner and invited herself.

Mom and Joy were making a salad, Mom rinsing lettuce while Joy chopped carrots, cucumbers, and tomatoes. Mom's phone rang, and she excused herself. Dad was out on the back porch grilling shrimp and chicken. Aunt Lil was sitting on the kitchen counter, feet dangling over the edge as she sipped a glass of wine.

Her bangles jangled as, holding her glass of wine in one hand, she rooted around in her bag with the other. Finally, she drew out a handful of red stones.

"Red Jasper," she explained. "The stones promote emotional stability. They may help Johnny ground himself in this difficult time."

She handed the stones to Ray.

"Gee, thanks, Aunt Lil," he said.

"Make sure Johnny gets them and carries them with him at all times. At night, he should place them under his pillow."

"Got it," Ray said.

"What are you going to do about Johnny?" I asked Ray. Then quickly added, for Aunt Lil's benefit: "Apart from the Red Jasper stones, of course."

He shrugged. "I don't know yet. Roxie says he needs to show he really wants the job at the Breeze. I know he needs it. But she's right—he doesn't act as if he does."

Roxie was staying home with Wimsey tonight. But she'd urged Ray to join the rest of the family for dinner. No doubt she thought it would give Ray some space to think—and maybe his parents and siblings would push him to make a decision.

From the dining room, I heard Mom let out a loud curse. As she strode back into the kitchen, she shoved her cell phone back into her pocket. She rejoined Joy at the kitchen table, continuing her work on the salad.

"Everything all right?" I asked.

"That judge denied my request for a search warrant."

"For where?"

She glanced at me, wariness creeping into her look. "Concordia House."

"Interesting," I said and moved closer to her.

"Not interesting enough. Or the judge would've agreed to issue the warrant." She sighed. "And this is the second time it's been denied. First, it was because of a clerical error —Deputy Douglas put in the address of Concordia House but failed to specify that the warrant was exclusively for Iggy's own room. Then, after I resubmitted, the judge dismisses the warrant request citing the Fourth Amendment."

"The Fourth Amendment?"

Mom nodded. "He said I failed to prove conclusively that Iggy's private room may hold key evidence in a crime that was committed at a different location."

"What if you try a third time?" I suggested. "Third time's a charm, and all that."

"I don't think I'll convince the judge." She wiped her hands on a piece of kitchen roll. "I'd better call Deputy Douglas. He and I were expecting the search warrant to come through. We even got a key from Mona and were going to head over to Concordia House tonight or tomorrow morning. It's good timing, because Concordia is empty. Mona, her team, and the halfway-house clients are at a retreat at the White Pine Monastery. The Buddhist monks host them a few times a year for therapeutic meditation and mindfulness. They'll be back at Concordia tomorrow after-noon." She sighed. "Anyway, it would've been good timing..."

She left the kitchen, and a moment later, I could hear her talking on the phone. But I couldn't hear what she was saying. I got busy helping the others prepare the food.

"Aunt Lil," I said at one point. "Hand me the salad tongs, will you?"

I turned and saw that Aunt Lil was gone. Where did she go?

Mom returned from her talk with Deputy Douglas. We finished preparing the salad and the corn, and then Dad walked in with a platter heaped with grilled shrimp and chicken.

"Let's eat!"

"Where's Aunt Lil?" I asked.

"I'm right here," Aunt Lil said, as she sauntered into the kitchen.

We moved into the dining room, where there was more space. Scottie sat on my left and Joy was pulling out the chair on my right when Aunt Lil swept in, her bangles and necklaces jangling.

"Why don't you sit next to your mom," Aunt Lil whispered. "You have such good energy, and your mom needs to clear that negativity from her aura."

"Oh," Joy said. "Good idea."

"And here—take these," Aunt Lil said, handing Joy a bunch of crystals.

Then she sat down next to me.

The platters of food got passed around. Beer and wine were served. And the conversation flowed freely. As I was eating my corn, Aunt Lil leaned close to me and her voice dropped to a murmur.

"I accidentally happened to overhear your mother on the phone," she said with a grin.

I glanced at her.

"She mentioned to her deputy that they'd been ready to go into Concordia with a search warrant," Aunt Lil continued. "And a key."

"Sure," I said. "She mentioned that."

"Well, apparently—" Aunt Lil straightened up, suddenly interested in cutting her chicken.

Down at the end of the table, Mom was looking our way.

Loudly, Aunt Lil said, "Fred, the chicken is grilled to perfection."

"Thanks, Lil," Dad said.

A moment later, Ray and Mom were in conversation, and Aunt Lil leaned close again.

"The key to Concordia House," she whispered. "Your

mom was ready to jump, in case the judge approved the search warrant."

A smile spread across Aunt Lil's face. A self-satisfied Cheshire cat grin.

"Aunt Lil," I whispered. "What did you do?"

She dug into her bag. When she pulled her hand, it was clenched in a fist. She opened it under the table, where only I could see.

She held a key in her hand.

I looked at her. "You stole it?"

"Borrowed it," Aunt Lil said. "We'll put it back in your mom's bag as soon as we can."

"We?"

She nodded. Her grin going even wider. "The planetary alignment is just right. Gates are opening for us. And now we have a key. It's only right that we use it."

I couldn't argue with that.

26

A soft lamp glowed behind the reception counter. Maybe someone left it on for safety's sake. To make it look as if someone might be around. But Concordia House, with its deep shadows, felt abandoned.

Aunt Lil and I stepped inside, and I closed the front door behind us and locked it. A vending machine in a corner hummed softly. Its lights had gone out. Maybe it did so automatically to conserve energy.

I turned and saw someone standing in the shadows. I drew in a sharp breath.

"It's just Jesus," Aunt Lil said.

"Oh," I said, letting out a breath of relief. "You're right."

The Jesus statue stood in the shadows, gazing kindly at us. He made me feel a little guilty about what we were doing, and I quickly moved past him.

Down a hallway, I glimpsed the cafeteria with its tiled floors and bare walls and rows of tables with folding chairs. A room near the check-in counter, its door left unlocked, revealed desks with old computers. No doubt a place residents could check their emails or search for jobs.

Aunt Lil tut-tutted. "They should lock these doors. Especially with all these computers. Burglars might break in, after all."

I glanced at her. No irony at all. No smile on her face acknowledging that we were the burglars.

She moved behind the reception counter. I followed her. A computer stood on the desk behind the counter. Aunt Lil shook the mouse, and the computer came out of its sleep. The screen demanded a password.

"Oh, crap," she said.

I rubbed a hand across my neck, thinking.

"Maybe it's 1, 2, 3, 4?" I suggested.

I tried it.

Incorrect password.

No luck. I wondered if only one person used the computer. Or if lots of different staff had access.

"If lots of staff need to remember a password…"

The desk had a top drawer. Aunt Lil pulled it out.

"Bingo," she said.

Inside was a purple sticky note that said,

PW: Concordia07

I typed in the password, unlocking the computer. Once I was inside the Concordia system, it didn't take me long to locate a folder with files on the residents.

And there it was: Ignatius Huxley.

I double clicked it. The file mentioned when Iggy had first come to Concordia. Multiple visits over the years. But it was a few months ago that he'd become a full-time resident. "Paid in full," it said for the months that he'd been staying at the center, and for the next month. "Private payment." Other entries said things like "nonprofit support" and "private donor payment."

Did Iggy have the money to pay for his stay at Concordia? It seemed unlikely. But there was no mention of who paid. The file also mentioned who Iggy's therapist was—Mona herself—and, importantly, which room he was staying in.

"Number 13," Aunt Lil said, shaking her head. "They put him in an unlucky room. What did they expect would happen?"

"Aunt Lil," I said. "Are you saying Iggy died because he stayed in an unlucky room?"

"I'm not not saying that's why he died." She raised a finger. "Keep an open mind."

I logged off the computer and we left the check-in area. We headed up the nearby stairwell. But as I put my hand on the railing, I stopped.

"Oh, no, what about fingerprints?"

I pulled back my hand.

"Relax," Aunt Lil said. "No one will know we've been here, and if anyone ever looked for prints, good luck. This place probably has dozens and dozens of fingerprints from all the people staying at Concordia. No need to worry."

I grabbed the railing again and continued to climb, hoping Aunt Lil was right.

On the first floor, halfway down the corridor, we found room 13. To my surprise, the doorknob turned smoothly, the door gliding inward.

"It's open," I said.

"Of course it is," Aunt Lil said. "I bet none of the doors have locks. For client safety."

We stepped into a narrow room and flicked on the light.

An overhead fluorescent tube flickered to life. An awful light.

Iggy's room had a single bed, a bedside table, and a sliver of a desk. A plastic folding chair. A closet stood crammed into a corner. A sink next to it. Guess the bathrooms were shared—and must be somewhere down the corridor.

A cup on the desk held a cluster of pens. I pulled out a few of the cheap ballpoint pens. About half were out of ink. Nothing else on the desk. Not even a sheet of paper.

Aunt Lil pulled open the bedside table's drawer.

"Batteries, tissues, and a stack of cards," she said.

I looked over her shoulder. A pack of Serenity Prayer cards lay in the drawer, the same as the kind I'd discovered down on the docks.

Next, I opened the closet. Highest up, shelves contained a few articles of clothing: t-shirts, underwear, socks, jeans, a sweater. Below that hung a threadbare jean jacket on a hanger. It had a few patches sewn onto the shoulders and chest, including ones that said Alice Cooper, Kiss, and Black Sabbath.

"Good taste in music," Aunt Lil said.

I looked at her. "Don't tell me you listen to heavy metal."

"Alice Cooper is hardly heavy metal." She smiled. "Besides, everyone lets their hair down when they're young and reckless."

She flicked her hair over her shoulders, as if to show that her hair was still down. Her necklaces and bangles jangled. She didn't need to convince me she still had a reckless streak—considering the fact that she'd encouraged me to break into Concordia House.

I searched the closet. Nothing else. Iggy must only have owned the one pair of shoes—the ones he died in.

I looked around. Iggy hadn't left much behind. Even if

Mom's warrant had come through, she might have come away empty-handed.

My eyes drifted over the desk again.

"Funny," I said.

"What, Alice Cooper?"

"No, Aunt Lil. Iggy. He used a bunch of pens. But there's no paper. So what did he write on?"

I crouched down by the desk and looked underneath. Felt around. Nothing.

Then, still sitting on my haunches, I turned and noticed the bed. A simple metal cot with a foam mattress and bedding. I inched closer. Squeezed a hand between the metal cot and the mattress and rooted around.

My hand struck something hard. Not metal. I closed my fingers around it and pulled it out.

What emerged from the hiding place under the mattress was a notebook. Not the expensive kind that I have a weakness for (and which I buy again and again at stationery and book stores, never to fill with any words). This was a simple black-marble composition notebook. It made me think of school.

Then I saw what Iggy had written on the front.

Iggy Huxley. Journal.

My gut clenched like a fist.

"This is it," I said.

"Wonderful," Aunt Lil said and clapped.

"Oh, great. This may be a key piece of evidence, and I just put my fingerprints all over it."

"Well, it's too late now, Park. We might as well take a closer look."

I flipped open the notebook, eager to read. Dense handwriting filled the lines on the paper. This was it. Iggy's thoughts put down on paper.

I heard something. I looked up. Aunt Lil's eyes widened. She'd heard it too.

"Footsteps," she hissed. "Someone's coming."

27

My heart flew into my throat. A soft thud-thud-thud was coming down the hallway. Someone was heading this way. In less than a minute, we'd be caught.

"The overhead light," I said.

I leaped to my feet and flicked the light switch. The room plummeted into darkness. My heart thundered. My breath sounded like a gale-force wind. Beyond my own sounds, the footsteps kept coming closer. And closer.

"I can't see," Aunt Lil muttered.

I looked at the bed. No way we'd fit under that. Beneath the desk? That was no hiding place.

"The closet," I whispered and reached out and grabbed Aunt Lil's hand in the dark.

I pulled open the closet door, shoved aside the jean jacket, and Aunt Lil squeezed into the tiny space.

"We can't both fit," I whispered.

"We'll have to. Now get in and close that door."

I climbed in and sat down, wedging myself into the tiny space between the wall and Aunt Lil. Then eased the door closed. I hugged my knees to my chest. The notebook pressed against my legs and my chin touched its hard cover. The darkness in the room had been a mild gloom compared with this blackness. But I welcomed it. The darker it was, the more hidden I felt. I could hear Aunt Lil's soft breathing.

From within the closet, I could no longer hear the footsteps.

"Can you hear anything?" I whispered.

"Maybe they passed the room," Aunt Lil whispered back. "Maybe we're safe."

The door to Iggy's room opened, silencing us. A flash of light underneath the closet door. Then darkness. But less deep now. A flashlight scanning the room?

The drawer in the bedside table opening and shutting. The scrape of the chair against the floor as the person moved it. Then the creak of the bed. The rustle of the bedding. The thump of the mattress, as the person apparently lifted it, and then dropped it again. Another thump.

The person must be looking for something.

The notebook. I pressed it closer to my chest.

The footsteps approached the closet. The light grew brighter. The gap under the closet door widened as it began to open.

Oh God, please, no.

Then a voice in the hallway: "Hello? Is someone there?"

The closet door snapped shut. The footsteps thudded on the floor. The door to room 13 clicked open.

"Hey," a voice called. "What're you doing here?" And then: "Stop!"

The footsteps, which had been too faint to hear from the closet before, were loud and clear now as they pounded down the corridor. The person was running—pursued by the person who'd called out.

The footsteps of the two people grew distant.

When I heard no more, I slipped out of the closet. I reached in and gave Aunt Lil my hand, helping her to get to her feet.

Opening the door quietly, I peered into the hallway. The two people—whoever they were—had run in the opposite direction from the stairwell.

"Come on," I whispered to Aunt Lil behind me. "We've got to get out—and fast."

We backtracked, moving as swiftly as we could toward the exit. As I hurried down the stairwell, I realized I was still clutching Iggy's journal. Not great. I wanted to read it and then replace it. Now I'd put my fingerprints all over the evidence and removed it from the scene. Mom wouldn't be impressed.

I'd have to worry about Mom later. First, Aunt Lil and I needed to get out undiscovered.

I reached the bottom of the stairs and flew into the reception area, aiming for the front door. Aunt Lil came jangling after me. I wished she'd left her jewelry at home. I unlocked the front door and pulled it open. Aunt Lil and I stepped outside. Closing the door again, I quickly locked it, and then turned around.

"Parker? Lil?"

I froze. I sensed Aunt Lil go rigid next to me.

In the dim light of the street lamp stood a familiar figure. Mona Macintosh.

A look of surprise on her face. Then she saw the key in my hand, and her wide-eyed surprise turned to a deep frown.

"I hope you two have a good explanation for this," she said.

I hoped we did, too.

28

Mona sat across from us at a formica-topped table in the Concordia House cafeteria. Paper cups of decaf coffee in front of us: Mona, Aunt Lil, and me. The smell of our coffee—reminding me of a whiff of burned wood—mingled with a pungent odor of disinfectant so strong it tingled in my eyes. At the center of the table lay the black-marble-covered notebook. I'd placed the key to Concordia House on top of it.

"I see," Mona said, after my honest explanation of why I'd been snooping around the recovery center at night. I'd also explained I had no idea who the fourth person was, only that they seemed to be looking for the notebook.

Mona touched her necklace, fiddling with the pearls. I wondered whether they were real or not. She said, "So you were willing to disregard the Fourth Amendment to get what you wanted? More importantly, you disregarded Iggy's privacy. Which he's entitled to, even in death."

I wrapped my hands around my paper coffee cup and stared at the black liquid.

"Guess that sums it up," I muttered, too ashamed to look Mona in the eye.

"And tell me why I shouldn't call your mom? Heck, maybe I should call the state police, since your mom has a clear conflict of interest."

I looked up. "Please, don't get her into trouble. It wasn't her fault."

"In fact," Aunt Lil said, "it was my fault. Parker wouldn't be here if it weren't for me. She protested." I glanced at Aunt Lil. But my aunt wasn't looking at me. She was gazing at Mona, apparently warming up to another classic performance. "Parker said to me, 'This is not right. We're better than this.' But I insisted that the ghost of poor Iggy demanded and deserved retribution, so he can rest in peace."

Mona eyed me. Like she thought Aunt Lil was nuts, and she was looking for someone sane. I shrugged. Mona turned one of the pearls on her necklace, spinning it around on its axis again and again. A nervous gesture. Like fiddling with a rosary.

"If I report you, you'll no doubt think I'm doing it to get back at you," Mona said.

"What?" It wasn't what I'd expected her to say. Not by a long shot. "Get back at me?"

"Well, not you. The Lee family. Or at least Ray."

She gave me a long look. I remembered what I'd learned about her past. Crazy Mona. And heat spread across my face.

"I wouldn't think that," I said.

"I know what people used to call me," she said. "Crazy Mona."

"I don't—"

Aunt Lil cut in: "Oh, you're Crazy Mona. I always wondered about that."

I groaned. So much for keeping that old story under wraps.

Mona dropped her necklace. "This can't be the first time you've heard my old nickname. Everyone has. And the fact is that I deserved it. I was obsessed with Ray back then. He was like my religion. He became the object of my devotion, and it wasn't a healthy dynamic. Needless to say." She shrugged. "But once I found my career and then my husband—and frankly, a renewed belief in God—my devotion found appropriate objects."

"You sound like you've given this some thought," I said.

"Not just me. My therapist, too." She chuckled. "Early on, I didn't want to let go of my unhealthy devotion. After all, it was my raft in the river. It held me up. But I had an inkling that sooner or later, the raft would come apart and I'd drown. I needed to get to the shore. So I got help. And I started swimming. I'm on dry land now. I'm happy now."

She smiled. She radiated a confidence and calm that I could only admire. How could someone go through such a transformation—from "Crazy Mona" to a woman who clearly "had it together"? I thought of Iggy, who'd tried to swim to the riverbank, but apparently failed. And I wondered about whoever murdered him. Was it someone who was stuck on a raft of their own, desperately battling the currents?

Aunt Lil reached into her bag and brought out her moonstone wand and waved it at Mona. Then, putting the stick back into her bag, she nodded. "I thought so. You have an exceptionally strong and clear and *healthy* aura. Good for you."

"It's late." Mona downed the rest of her coffee and put a hand on the notebook and the key. "I'll be taking these."

"But if the notebook can shed light on how Iggy died?" I said.

She shook her head. "It contains personal stuff. Deeply personal stuff. That has nothing to do with the burglary at the Breeze. We've got to respect that Iggy used his journal to process his pain. It was part of therapy. Never meant for others to read."

I bit my lip. Gave her a single nod. She was right, of course. But while my mind told me she was justified in holding onto the journal, my hands tingled with an antsy desperation to grab the notebook and flip through the pages. Find the truth.

I sighed, letting my agitation go with my breath. I drained the rest of my coffee, the bitter taste feeling appropriate. The moment had, after all, left a bitter taste in my mouth.

Mona got up. She pocketed the key and tucked the notebook under her arm.

Aunt Lil finished her coffee, too. All three of us—one by one—deposited our empty cups in the trash.

As we walked through the cafeteria, with its stark white tiles, I said, "The other person—are you sure you didn't recognize them?"

"They wore a hood, and I didn't get close enough." She shook her head. "What are the chances that another person would break into Concordia House on the same night you did?"

I'd given this some thought already.

"Pretty good, actually. Usually, this place is busy. But hearing you were gone on a retreat, I saw an opportunity. The other person must've too."

"We always have a person on duty at night, in case someone drops in. Even if we are on retreat."

"Which is why you showed up."

"That's right."

We left the cafeteria behind and Mona guided me through a door and into an office. Obviously hers. A framed degree in social work hung on the wall. Another revealed she'd studied psychology. The walls also featured framed photos of events at Concordia House. Some of staff and clients in the woods, hiking, or at a picnic. Lots of smiling faces.

Mona made a beeline for a wall safe behind her desk. She turned the knob until it clicked, and she opened the safe. She put the notebook inside. Then locked the safe again.

I let out another sigh. Now there was no way I'd find out what the notebook contained, unless Mom worked some miracle and got the judge to change his mind about the warrant.

Mona led Aunt Lil and me out of the office, through the reception, and opened the front door to let us out. I passed through, ready to head home to Broadstairs House to get a few hours of sleep before another day began. Aunt Lil said goodnight and began to walk down the street. On a nearby lamppost, a poster advertising the Breeze had been torn to shreds, leaving only a sliver of Ray's smiling face and the word "Restaurant."

"Parker," Mona said, stopping me.

I turned around. So did Aunt Lil.

Mona hesitated. Then said, "I know what's in the notebook. I was Iggy's therapist, after all." She drew in a deep breath. "I can't believe I'm sharing this. But I do think Iggy would be fine with it."

My heart trilled with excitement. "Fine with what?"

"In the notebook, Iggy expresses frustration with this situation. He didn't just tell me. He told others at Concordia House, too, which is why I feel all right sharing it."

"Frustration?"

"I learned this later, and honestly, if he'd been aboveboard about it from the beginning, I would've intervened. I might even have said no."

"Said no to Iggy?"

"No, sorry. I'm not being clear." Mona shook her head. "I mean, I would've said no to Lester."

"Lester?" My heart clenched in my chest. "His brother?"

"That awful man," Aunt Lil added.

"Sure," Mona said. "Lester paid for Iggy's stay. I found out after Iggy joined us that it was against his will. He was coerced by Lester into coming. Recently, he told me he wanted out—out from under his brother's thumb—and he said he'd found a way."

"What way?"

Mona shook her head. "I don't know. But it must've been about money. And Lester must've known. Because he withdrew his support."

"He what?"

"Yeah," Mona said with a grimace. "He stopped payments. If Iggy had lived, his stay at Concordia House would've come to an end."

29

The wine bar was still officially closed, but the shutters were up. Outside, tables and chairs set up, wiped down, all ready for the day. Apparently, Lester liked to get things ready early. Maybe because he expected another busy day.

I knocked on the door.

Through the glass in the door, I could make out a shadowy figure ambling toward me. Then Lester's bald head and hard stare materialized out of the gloom. He unlocked the door and opened it.

"What do you want?"

"I want to ask you about Iggy."

"No, thanks."

He shut the door. But I caught it with my foot. The edge of the door dug into the side of my shoe. Ouch. He kept pushing, and the door dug down to my skin and bone. Painful. But I forced my face to remain calm. Stony.

"I know about Concordia House," I said.

Lester stopped shoving the door shut. Which was a relief

for my foot. But he didn't open it. "So what? Is it a crime now to pay for your brother's rehab?"

"I also know you were going to stop payments."

He stared at me. "Get out of here," he said in a low voice.

"In another couple of weeks," I said, pressing on, "Iggy would've been evicted. He would've been back out on the streets. Thanks to you."

"Thanks to me?" Lester yanked the door open. "It was thanks to me that good-for-nothing parasite got a room at Concordia. And trust me, I would've been fine if he'd been rotting in the streets of Chicago, L.A., or New York. In the big city, people wouldn't look at him and think, 'Look at what the Huxleys have come to. Look how far they've sunk.'"

Wow, he really believed that. How many people in Allington cared about what the Huxleys had come to? Sure, our town had plenty of busybodies and moralists, but most folks would've been concerned about Iggy, not judgmental about the family.

Lester continued: "But Iggy stuck close to home. He insisted on doing things his way. He didn't have an ounce of respect for authority or decency. Only for the next high. Which is why, no doubt, he wanted out. He wanted to leave Concordia, and on his own terms, too."

"What do you mean—his own terms?"

"He wasn't going to walk out the next day. Oh, no. My spoiled little brother would wait until he had enough money to find a place to stay, and until then, he'd take advantage of my generosity. I might as well have paid for a hotel." He snorted. "Although Concordia is a heck of a lot cheaper than that overrated Lakeview Inn."

No doubt he knew Aunt Lil owned the Lakeview. But I let the insult slide.

"You said he was getting money to find a place of his own," I said. "How?"

Lester laughed. It was a flat, dry laugh. Like a sick dog. "He said he got a job. But when I asked him what kind of job it was, he became cryptic. Said it was something in the Food & Beverage industry. Of course, he was joking. Playing games. And in hindsight, I see he was referring to the sabotage at the Breeze. I told your mom all about this already." He frowned. "Don't think I don't know what you're all thinking. That I somehow sicced my brother on the Breeze. That I planned it all. But Iggy wasn't doing it out of respect for me. He didn't respect anyone. He did it to defy me."

Then something changed on Lester's face. Eyebrows lifting. Lips stretching. It almost looked like a smile. Only not as pleasant.

"Besides," he said. "I don't need sabotage to drive your brother out of business. I'll do it by running my business better than he could ever do. I'll take away his customers one at a time. You'll see. Before long, Ray will be begging me to buy the Breeze."

He laughed. Again that wheezy, dry bark.

Then he drew back his right leg and swung. Kicking my foot.

"Hey!"

I drew back. My foot was clear of the door, and he slammed it shut.

This time his smile, through the dark glass, was big and sincere. Like a little boy who just got an ice cream.

30

After spending a couple of hours at *The Gazette* writing an article on the best way to install hummingbird feeders, with insights from a handful of Allington natives, I hurried down to the docks again. Anxious. After Lester's confident pronouncement that he'd steal Ray's customers (he forgot to mention they were Roxie's, too), I was beginning to think he might be right. He was the businessman, after all. He must know things I didn't. Maybe the Breeze was already in a free fall. By the time I got there, I'd find empty tables everywhere.

All right, so the tables outside were full of happy diners. Tables overflowing with French fry baskets and burgers in butcher paper. Plus, frothy pints of beer.

But this might be an exception. It was a sunny day, after all, and it was lunchtime...

I stepped through the door.

Then let out my breath. I dropped my shoulders, the tension going out of them.

Customers occupied nearly every table, and there was an abundance of food out: Cobb salads, grilled chicken sandwiches, platters with cut veggies and dips. Glasses of beer, wine, soft drinks. Music was playing. Friends and couples talking. Laughing. There was a real buzz today. A buzz that said all was well at the Breeze.

Clearly, I didn't need to worry.

Sandra rushed past to take an order from a table. After she'd repeated the order to the customers, she spun around to head back to the bar. As she passed me, she gave me a big smile. "Come for lunch, Park?"

"Just to talk to Ray and Roxie."

"They're at the bar."

Sandra seemed to be thriving in her new job. I was happy to see it. Ray and Roxie needed good people.

But there was another server, too. And when he turned around, I stopped. Johnny Boudreau. He took orders from a couple, offering them a half-hearted smile. But at least it was a smile. He seemed to be keeping his anger in check.

I approached the bar, where Ray was filling a pint glass with club soda and ice. Roxie was talking to Sandra, handing her drinks for one of her tables.

"So we're on for the weekend?" Roxie said.

"You bet," Sandra said, a big smile on her face. "Can't wait."

"You're a lifesaver, Sandra. Ray and I really appreciate it."

Sandra shrugged. "And I appreciate the work. If it helps the Breeze..."

Roxie reached out and touched Sandra's arm, and Sandra flinched, as if it startled her. Roxie said, "It helps us. You know how Wimsey gets. We can't let that dog be alone for so long. With you taking care of him, Ray and I can focus on work. Heck, we'll even take some time for ourselves—a little romantic date."

Sandra smiled. A stiff smile. "That's nice."

Then, balancing a tray full of drinks, she moved off to serve her customers. I thought of her reaction at the gym.

Roxie must've made the same connection. She said, "Crap. I forgot. She's in a long-distance relationship. The last thing she wants to hear is about us finding time to go on a date."

"She'll be fine," Ray said.

I gave Ray a questioning look. "What's this about? Wimsey?"

He laughed. "Yeah, that dog is high maintenance. So Sandra's going to take him for the day. On her day off. Roxie and I anticipated we'd be far behind schedule this weekend, and so we've planned for both of us to be at the Breeze every day."

Roxie cut in. "But things are going well. Looks like we can take some of that extra time and go on a date instead. Goodness knows we can use a little quiet time together."

Ray nodded and ran a hand through his hair. "It's been an intense month."

"Speaking of intense, I see Johnny's back at work," I said.

"What can I say?" Ray said with a shrug. "I believe in second chances."

"Despite attitude problems."

"Despite that, yeah. But the guy's trying to do the right thing for his grandma. He just needs to learn that he's got friends around him who can help him do the right thing. We're not adversaries, we're allies."

Roxie passed behind Ray, heading toward the other end of the bar, where a customer was waiting. She said, "He actually told Johnny that—the thing about adversaries and allies." She smiled and touched Ray on the back of his neck.

Then continued on her way. "My hubby's one of the good guys," she said.

Ray glanced at her with a smile. Then set the club soda down in front of the customer at the bar.

It was Wally. He gave me a sheepish look. "Yeah, yeah, I know. I should've talked things through with Johnny and Ray, so this whole thing didn't escalate..." He took a sip of his drink. "I knew Johnny was doing a bad thing. I thought it would be all right. That I was helping Johnny and somehow that would help the Breeze. I got that totally wrong. And then Johnny couldn't really do all his work at the Zephyr Bar, anyway. He showed up late. And half the time he was too tired to focus." He shook his head. "I should've talked to Ray."

The door to the brewery in the back opened, and Dani emerged. She was wearing a face mask, which she took off. She must've been working with something smelly. She ran a hand across her brow. Smelly, sweaty work. Making beer wasn't easy. I was happy sticking with my words at *The Gazette*.

"Cold drink?" Ray asked.

Dani nodded, plonking down on a bar stool next to me. "Things are looking good. I've cleaned up, so we can get started early this weekend on the next batch."

"Good work." Ray served her a glass of water with ice. "We're catching up."

Dani grabbed her drink and swiveled around to gaze at the activity in the Breeze. She took a big sip of her water. Then crunched an ice cube between her teeth.

"Business is good," she said. "What a relief."

"Thanks to you all," Ray said. "None of this would be possible without you and Sandra and Johnny."

"We'll see about Johnny..."

"I'm willing to give him another chance," Ray said. "I think you should, too."

Dani nodded. "All right. We'll see…" Then she brightened. "But Sandra's great, isn't she? I don't know where she gets the energy. Volunteering at Concordia House with me. Serving at the Breeze."

"And dog sitting for Ray and Roxie," I added.

Dani laughed. "See? Endless energy."

Sandra came back to the bar to get more drinks. Ray lined them up.

"We're talking about you," Dani said, giving Sandra a little nudge. Then added, "Where do you get the energy from? How can you do three jobs at once?"

Sandra shrugged. "Nothing else to do. When I get my boyfriend back, things will be different. Everything will be different."

She glanced down, as if suddenly shy. As if looking us in the eye would embarrass her. She twirled the engagement ring on her finger. Then she grabbed the tray off the bar and hurried off to deliver the drinks.

I shook my head. "The work is one thing. The relationship is another. I couldn't handle doing a long-distance relationship like that."

Dani frowned. "Me either. But the thing is, sometimes I worry."

"Worry? About what?"

"I don't know. It's just—"

I looked at her with a raised eyebrow.

"Forget I said that," she added quickly. "Her love life is none of my business." She drained her glass. "Better get back to work."

31

The next morning, Saturday, I settled into my seat at *The Gazette* and opened my laptop. I had so little to go on. Iggy's death was still a mystery. But it still seemed that everything led back to the Huxleys. Maybe I'd missed some detail on the family.

I searched *The Gazette* archives. Looked through library databases. Other news media. But there wasn't much. A few old *Gazette* articles about the dad's military service and his involvement in the American Legion, and then a couple of mentions of Lester and his businesses. And zilch on Iggy.

Dad, leaning back in his chair, had his feet up on his desk. He was reading a well-worn copy of *The Snack Thief* by Andrea Camilleri, one of his favorite mystery authors. It was a slow day at work. Unlike other Saturdays, especially in summer, there were no major events in Allington to cover today.

"Dad," I said. "Got anything on the Huxleys that might be worth including in my article?"

He lowered his book and launched into a summary of what I'd already learned about Huxley Sr. and Lester.

"What about Iggy?"

"What about him? He's known around town as a drinker. Maybe he did other drugs, too. Occasionally, he'd appear to pull himself out. He'd get a job. Packing at the supermarket. Picking up litter. Mowing lawns." He paused and looked thoughtful. Then his bushy eyebrows shot up. "In fact, now I think of it, he even served as handyman and gardener for Roxie's family."

"Was he a good handyman and gardener?"

"I don't know. I always assumed it was out of charity that they hired him. But you'd better ask Roxie about that. Anyway, it didn't last long. Iggy had a falling out with Roxie's folks and stormed off. That was the end of that. And then Iggy was back on the bottle." He sighed and shook his head. "So sad. That kid didn't have an easy life."

I picked up my phone.

"Hey, Roxie," I said. "How about a cup of coffee?"

32

Roxie and I met at Cafe Larke. Saturdays at my sister Joy's cafe were always busy. Kids playing in the kids' corner. Grownups chatting over lattes. Despite the activity, it was a calm space. Lots of plants. A small tabletop fountain sat on the counter, its water trickling down. Framed prints of Julia Larke's impressionist paintings. Relaxing jazz played from overhead speakers. As I walked in, I recognized the song as one Dad often put on his vinyl record player: "So What" by Miles Davis.

Mona was sitting at a corner table with a Buddhist monk, shaved head and all, and she nodded at me as I entered. I waved. Feeling heat rise to my face. Guess I'd always feel embarrassed about being caught snooping around Concordia House. She'd been a good sport about it. No tattling to my mom. Although sooner or later, knowing myself, I'd be the one to tell Mom. I was lousy at keeping secrets from her.

Roxie stood by the counter, and when I called her name, she turned.

"Look at us," she said with a big smile, "meeting casually

for coffee. Such freedom. If it weren't for Sandra babysitting Wimsey, I'd be homebound right now."

"Instead, you're at the Breeze working."

She laughed. "You got me. But actually, Ray and I are going for a hike later today. Dani's got things under control at the brewery, and that's freed her up to work the bar and manage the servers. Things with Johnny are better. Thank goodness. So your brother and I are taking most of the day off."

"Good for you."

Joy was running a yoga class at her studio up Peony Lane, so it was Ashley who took our orders. We both got lattes to go. Roxie wanted to get back to Ray. And I wanted to get back to work.

As we waited for our coffees at the end of the counter, I told her about my attempts to learn more about Iggy. Roxie put a hand to her chest and said, "What a tragic end. Iggy got dealt a difficult hand."

"I heard he did some work for your family."

"That's right. Briefly."

Our coffees arrived. We thanked Ashley and walked out into the sunshine. The cafe tables outside were full. On the opposite corner of Peony and Main, Balthazar Books was open, with racks of used or discounted books set outside on the sidewalk to tempt passersby. Up Peony Lane, people were wandering in and out of Maxine's Maximum Beauty, Big Heart Stationery, and the many quaint little knickknack shops. Allington was buzzing with life.

But my mind was on death.

"So," I said, as we wandered down Main Street toward the crosswalk by the docks. "Iggy—he worked for your family."

Roxie nodded, took a sip of her coffee, and said, "Right.

Mom and Dad felt bad for him. They knew Huxley Sr., and so they wanted to help out."

"They were friends with Iggy and Lester's dad?"

"Not exactly, no. They knew him. They knew how tough he was on his boys. Like a drill sergeant. It seemed to work for Lester. But it broke Iggy."

I wondered about that—had it really "worked" for Lester? He seemed hard and bitter. Hardly proof of a positive upbringing.

We stopped at the crosswalk. The pedestrian signal was red. For a Saturday, Main Street was quiet—only an occasional car drifting past us. I was tempted to jaywalk, a habit from the big city, but in Allington people had more patience—they waited until the light changed.

Roxie continued, "The work wasn't much. They paid just above minimum wage for him to fix up a shed in the backyard and do some gardening. And it didn't last long, either. Iggy became dissatisfied with the work. Resentful. Kind of paranoid, too. He'd accuse them of saying things about him."

"Is that why he left?"

"He left because he demanded a raise. Which my parents were open to. But when they talked about it, his idea of a fair wage kept going up and up. One day he'd say an extra two bucks an hour. The next he'd say five. An hour later, it would be eleven. In the end, he demanded so much money, they couldn't in good faith say yes. He accused them of promising to double his wages. Which was pure fiction. Then he threatened to report them for hiring an illegal contractor."

"Wow, and did he?"

"No. He simply stormed off and never came back." She shook her head. "I don't think he was well, Park. My parents thought a job would fix things for Iggy, but Iggy needed more than a job. He needed help."

"He needed Concordia House."

Roxie nodded.

The light changed.

Roxie glanced left and right at the crosswalk and stepped off the curb.

A car revved its engine, and a screech of tires screamed. Out of the corner of my eye came a flash of red, flying straight at us.

"Roxie!"

I grabbed her arm and yanked. Her coffee tumbled out of her hand. Somewhere along the way, my own had vanished, and now I was gripping Roxie and pulling her down to the ground. The red car barreled past us, the air buffeting me, and I hit the sidewalk hard. Pain shot through me and I gritted my teeth.

Someone cried out. I heard the scraping of chairs. A man's voice calling out: "Hey!"

But my focus was on Roxie. I was still gripping her. We were lying side by side on the hard pavement, and she was staring at me, eyes wide with shock.

"Wha—wha—what happened?" she stuttered.

"Are you hurt?"

"I don't think so. No."

I sat up. Wrinkled my nose. An acrid stench filled my nostrils. Something burning. I turned and saw, right at my feet, a large piece of paper curling with fire, the smoke sending black tendrils into the air.

A crowd gathered around us, and a woman stepped into the street and started stamping on the burning paper. I stared at it. That wasn't paper. It was a poster. One of the many posters around town advertising the Breeze.

33

Ray crossed the Breeze, carrying a cup of coffee. He set it down on the table in the booth.

"Drink this," he told Roxie as he sat down next to her. He put a hand on her back.

"Coffee," she said, her voice flat.

"Coffee with a dash of love."

"Coffee with a dash of love" was Ray's euphemism for added bourbon. But nobody needed to explain that to Roxie. She was married to the man.

Mom leaned across the table and pushed the cup closer to Roxie, encouraging her to drink. "You'll feel better after this," she said.

Roxie lifted the coffee to her lips and slurped it, gulping down half of it in one swallow.

"Easy, sweetie," Ray said, rubbing her back. "It's got a big dash of love."

"It's good," she said.

Then her eyes went wild, and she put the cup down with a bang.

"Wimsey," she said.

"Wimsey's fine, remember? He's with Sandra. Back at home."

"Oh." She pressed a hand to her forehead. "I don't know why I got scared. All of a sudden, I thought Wimsey was the one in trouble."

"It's shock," Mom said. "It's normal."

"Still, I'd like Wimsey to be here."

"I'll get him," Ray said and got up. "I'll be right back."

Mom said, "Roxie, what you need is peace and quiet, and some rest." She heaved a sigh. "But I can't give you that yet. I need to know what you saw." She glanced sideways at me. "And you, too, Park."

Roxie shook her head. "I was crossing the street, that was all. And then a car came out of nowhere. Park, she—" She looked at me. "You saved my life."

I shrugged. "I needed to get out of the way. Thought I'd better take you with me."

"Did you recognize the car?" Mom asked.

I stared down at the table. The sidewalk had scraped the side of my left hand, leaving it raw and red. Red. The car had been red. I narrowed my eyes, almost closing them, trying to conjure an image of the vehicle as it flashed past us.

A red Toyota Camry.

I looked at Mom. Then I stared off toward the bar.

Johnny Boudreau stopped by our booth with a pitcher of ice water.

"More water?" he said in his usual gruff manner. Then, softening, he added, "Can I get you anything, Roxie?"

Roxie shook her head.

"Hey, Johnny," I said. "Where's Dani?"

He shrugged. "Busy out back in the brewery, I guess. Cleaning, probably. Me and the others had things under control in the restaurant, so she stepped out."

I got up. My legs felt shaky as I headed toward the back. What if I found the brewery empty? What if Dani wasn't at the Breeze?

"What's going on?" Mom asked behind me. "Where are you going?"

I strode past empty tables and past some with customers enjoying a drink or the remnants of a late lunch. At the back, I ignored the sign on the door that told us civilians to keep out ("DANGER: Staff Only"), yanked it open, and stepped inside.

The brewery, with its massive vats, hummed. Somewhere, something dripped. But the emptiness felt immense. I wandered down the tiled floor. My heart beating fast.

"Hello?"

As I entered the area with the fermentation tanks, where the ceiling shot upward, I noticed how neat everything was. Sure didn't look like it needed cleaning. I moved past the metal stairs leading to the landing above.

And then heard a clank.

I looked up, my heart flying into my throat.

Dani was sitting on the metal walkway above. Sitting cross-legged with a wrench in her hand. Staring straight at me.

"Oh, it's you," she said with a sigh.

"Yeah, it's me."

I went back and climbed the stairs. I reached the top, and some small part of me—the anxious knot in my stomach—still expected Dani to come flying at me with that wrench.

But she didn't. She continued to sit, fiddling with the adjustable wrench. And looking deeply unhappy.

"What's going on?" I asked cautiously.

"I don't know if I can do it," she mumbled. "I thought it didn't matter. I thought I could get past how I felt about him and just do my work. Not get emotional. But it's hard. I guess I still have feelings for him."

My head spun. "Wait, what? Are you talking about Ray?"

She looked up, her eyes widening. "Ray? Jeez, what would make you think that?"

"Then who—?" A flash of insight. The pieces came together, and part of the puzzle suddenly made sense. "Johnny."

Dani nodded. "We used to, you know..."

"The two of you were serious," I said. "Serious enough for Johnny to tattoo your initial on his arm. I didn't question why the lettering for 'grandma' looked so different from the D. But I get it now."

"Yeah, he added 'grandma' to the tattoo. After he broke up with me." Something caught in her throat. Then she said, with bitterness in her voice, "Luckily, her name is Dominique, so he didn't have to have the tattoo removed. He could just add to it. Wasn't that convenient?" She sighed. "Listen to me. I sound awful. Because he really does love his grandma. And she really is great."

It all made sense. This was why Dani had been so angry with Johnny. Not that Johnny hadn't acted terribly—he had —but Dani, unlike Ray, wasn't interested in giving him a second chance, because he'd hurt her. Hurt her deeply.

I wanted to help her get past this. But I couldn't spend time on Dani's heartbreak. Not right now.

I crouched down to get closer to her.

"Dani," I said. "I'd love to talk to you about Johnny. But it'll have to wait. I need your help."

Dani looked up. Clearly noticing the seriousness in my voice. She frowned.

"What happened, Park? And how can I help?"

34

"See," Dani said. "It's right here, where I left it."

We were standing in the municipal parking lot and looking at her red Toyota Camry. And I was feeling foolish. How many old red Toyota Camrys must there be in the world?

I rubbed the back of my neck. "It just seemed like a big coincidence."

"You didn't think somehow I—?" Dani frowned. Her reprimand was sharp. "Parker Lee, how could you?"

"I'm sorry, Dani. Guess the shock of what happened got to me, too."

Dani eyed me. Then nodded and put a hand on my arm. Giving me a gentle squeeze. "It must've been awful. I'm glad you and Roxie are OK."

I nodded. "Me too. Let's go back to the Breeze."

"Sure. Let me just grab my cap."

She unlocked the car on the passenger side, leaned in, and retrieved a baseball cap. She paused, leaving the door open. She wrinkled her nose.

"What the—? That's strange."

She bent down, as if she were looking for something in the car.

"What's wrong?" I asked.

"That smell..."

I wedged myself next to her and stuck my head inside the car. She was right. There was a distinctive whiff of something like alcohol. And something burned.

"What's this doing here?"

She reached down to pick up an object underneath the front passenger seat.

"No," I said, grabbing her by the arm. "Don't touch that."

She pulled back. Both of us standing straight outside the open passenger-side door. She said, "Why? What is it?"

"Lighter fuel," I said. "And it's evidence."

"Evidence?"

"I bet this was used to set fire to that poster."

Dani's mouth turned into an O of surprise. "You mean someone stole my car? They stole my car and tried to run you and Roxie down?"

I nodded.

"But how?"

Dani looked around the parking lot, as if the culprit might be lurking near us. A group of pigeons pecked at something near a bench. The trees nearby rustled gently in the breeze. No culprit here.

"The person must've broken into the car," she said.

I ran a finger along the edge of the window. No scrapes. No signs of slim-jimming, where the thief put a thin piece of wire or flat metal between the window and the rubber seal in the door to pick the lock. I went around the car and checked the other side. No scrapes there, either.

"No shattered windows and no lock-picking," I said, leaning against the roof of the car and looking across at

Dani. "And your car's too old for a thief to mess with a lock signal."

She snorted. "The only signal my car gives is in winter when it refuses to start." Then she frowned. "But how could the person get into my car, then?"

"A key."

"The only key is mine," Dani said and patted her pocket. "Oh, and the spare one at home."

Then her eyes widened.

"Oh, no. You think someone broke into my place?"

Ice was spreading in my gut. My head throbbed with images. The Breeze. Sabotaged tank. Iggy dead on the floor. I couldn't piece the entire puzzle together yet, but most of the pieces were fitting. And it made me shudder.

At this point, a break-in at Dani's would be a relief.

"Come on," I said. "We've got no time to lose."

35

Dani's apartment was on the 3rd floor of a brick building. She unlocked the front door, glanced at me nervously, and then pushed it open. I was about to step inside when Mom grabbed me by the shoulder.

"Deputy Douglas goes in first," she said.

"Yes, ma'm," he said and squeezed past us.

I'd called Mom from the municipal lot, and she'd told us to leave the car, lock it, and she'd pick us up. Dani's car was now evidence, part of a crime investigation. And we should all go to her apartment together. It was time to close this case.

But that assumed we'd find anything at Dani's place.

Deputy Douglas disappeared down the short hallway and into the living room. I could see him peering into a bedroom. Then continuing to the next. Peering inside.

He turned around and shrugged.

"All right," Mom said. "Let's all go inside."

Dani went first, then I followed, and Mom brought up the rear.

The apartment bore signs of fancier times: crown molding that had been painted over hundreds of times, nearly erasing their features, and hardwood floors that had deep gouges and ugly stains.

Dani's furniture was simple. There was a small couch, a TV, and a hutch with plates and glasses. Down the hallway was an eat-in kitchen with table and chairs.

But my interest was in the bedrooms. Dani headed into her own, the first, and rummaged through a drawer in a desk. I waited in the doorway. She turned toward me, shaking her head.

"It's not here."

"You're sure that's where you left it?"

"I'm sure."

Mom was examining the windows. Deputy Douglas was, too. He tapped the window in the kitchen and said, "This one's the obvious one. The fire escape is out there. But the window's shut tight. We should consider that—"

"No," Dani said. "It must be a burglar."

"All right—first, let's rule out that possibility," Mom said.

While they continued to look for signs of a break-in, I slipped into the other bedroom, Sandra's.

Simple. Neat. A single bed with the covers pulled down tight. A desk with no clutter. A framed photograph of a handsome guy in a navy uniform. A corkboard above that with two more photos. One of an aircraft carrier. Another of the same handsome guy but in close-up. I leaned close to the photo, studying it.

"That's Sandra's fiancé," Dani said, coming up behind me.

"It's the same photo."

"What do you mean?"

"This second one—" I touched the one on the corkboard. "—it's a cropped version of the framed one. Does she have any other photos?"

Dani shrugged. "I don't go snooping around her stuff. Not my style. And she's made it clear she values her privacy. Her door's usually closed. But she's got a photo album I often see her looking at."

I turned around, looking for the photo album. A small bookshelf contained about a dozen books. Urban fantasy books. Shapeshifter romance novels. The Bible. But no photo album.

Mom appeared in the doorway behind Dani.

"What's on your mind, Park?"

"Probably nothing..."

That icy feeling in my gut only got colder. I went to the bed and crouched down. Shoved a hand into the gap between the mattress and the bed frame and rooted around.

"Hello..."

I felt something hard. I grasped it and pulled it out.

"The photo album," Dani said. Then frowned. "But why would she hide it?"

I sat on the bed, and even before opening it, I knew.

As I flipped the pages, my limbs turned cold. I shuddered.

The first photo showed a young Sandra with her boyfriend, his arm around her shoulders. They were both smiling. And of course I knew who the boyfriend was.

It was Ray.

I let out a groan.

I flipped to the next page.

More photos of Sandra and Ray.

I flipped the page. More photos. But now they were just of Ray. Half-torn photos with hints of another person who'd been ripped out of the picture—an arm, a strand of hair, or even half a jaw, the only thing remaining. I recognized a photo that I'd seen before—one from *The Gazette*—of Ray and Roxie together in front of the Breeze. But Roxie had been torn out of the picture. And I thought of the vandalized Breeze posters around town, and how Ray's face remained intact in each of them.

Across the top of each page, Sandra had written with thick marker pen:

NEVER LET GO. NEVER LET GO. NEVER LET GO.

"My God," Mom said. I hadn't even noticed her approach. She was standing next to me, looking down at the photo album. "She's obsessed."

I looked up at Mom.

"Ray," I said. "He went back home to get Wimsey. Sandra's there."

Mom's eyes narrowed. "Let's go."

36

Ray and Roxie's house looked peaceful. A lawn sprinkler waved calmly back and forth, flicking water into the sun and making a little rainbow. A dog toy—a chewy bone—lay in the grass and I picked it up as Mom and I strode toward the front door. A dozen feet or so away, Deputy Douglas was pressing himself into the narrow gap between the house and the neighboring hedge to get to the backyard.

Mom stopped at the front door.

"What do we do," I asked, "knock?"

She dug a key out of her pocket and dangled it for me to see. "Moms always have a spare."

She fitted the key in the lock and carefully—I gritted my teeth, waiting for a loud click—she turned it and then eased the door open.

She held a finger to her lips.

"I know," I whispered.

I leaned against the doorframe, lifted my left foot, and grabbed the heel of my sneaker.

"What are you doing?" Mom hissed.

"Taking my shoes off."

"Why are you taking your shoes off?"

"Going barefoot. It's more quiet. Like a ninja."

Mom nudged me. She nodded at the hallway ahead of us. I looked. The floor was covered in deep carpeting.

"Uh," I said. "Right."

I pressed my shoe back on.

As soon as we'd stepped inside, Mom eased the door shut. The hallway stretched down to the kitchen. Chewed-up magazines and ripped-apart paperback novels lay scattered across the carpeted floor. Wimsey's work. Like he'd gone a little crazy when Sandra left him alone—when she'd trekked across town to "borrow" Dani's car.

The living and dining room was off to the left. The door to the basement on the right. Bedrooms upstairs.

Muffled voices came through the floor from downstairs.

"The basement," Mom said.

She motioned for me to open the door to the basement. I turned the knob as slowly and quietly as I could, and she stepped through. I slid through the doorway, following close behind.

More thick carpeting—thank goodness—covered the stairs leading down into the basement. We tiptoed down. Halfway down, Mom stopped. From ahead of us came a strange sound. A sharp rattle.

"One false move," Sandra said, "and it's dead."

Mom glanced back at me, a look of horror on her face. She put a hand on her holster and eased her gun out.

We continued down. At the bottom, the stairs hit the low landing, where we turned into the basement's long room.

And there it was: exercise bike, pool table, and beyond them, the man-cave bar. I stood stock-still. Mom slid her gun back into its holster.

Ray was sitting on a stool, and Sandra was behind the bar. Wimsey, I saw with relief, lay at Ray's feet.

But what the heck was going on?

In front of Sandra was a chopping board with a knife and wedges of lime and lemon. Several bottles, too, including gin and a small brown one that looked like medicine. She held up a shaker and shook it, the ice inside rattling. Then she took off the top and poured a frothy concoction into a cocktail glass.

"Looks great," Ray said, reaching for the glass. "Let me try it, so we can get going. I don't want to keep Roxie waiting any longer."

Sandra frowned. "Hold on. There's a final step."

"Sandra, I'm sorry, but I really can't—"

"Just this last detail and it's done."

She grabbed a bottle of club soda, undid the cap, and poured a dash into the shaker. Then swirled it and dribbled the liquid into the cocktail.

"Presto," she said. "A perfect Ramos Gin Fizz, the hardest cocktail of them all."

Then she looked up and saw us.

"Oh," she said. "Chief Lee. Parker."

Wimsey raised his head, looking our way. For a second, I worried he'd spring into action and come bounding toward us. What if it somehow set Sandra off? We had no idea what she was capable of.

Actually, we did. She'd murdered Iggy and tried to run Roxie down. She'd spent years obsessing about her ex-boyfriend Ray, inventing a fake fiancé as a cover for her fixation.

Ray turned on the stool. "Hey—sorry for taking so long. Did you come to get me? See, Sandra insisted on showing me her bartending skills." He swiveled back to Sandra. "Here, let me taste so we can get going."

He reached for the cocktail.

"No," Mom said, taking a step forward. "Stop. Don't touch that, Ray. It may contain poison."

"Poison?" Sandra said.

Mom pointed to the small brown bottle.

"That's orange flower water, Mom," Ray said. "It's for the cocktail."

Sandra frowned. "Who do you think I am? I'd never in a million years poison Ray."

I stepped forward.

"You're right," I said, and pointed the dog toy at her, wagging it along with my accusation. "You'd never hurt Ray. You're still in love with him."

"What?" Ray looked at Sandra, and then back at me. He shook his head. "Don't be crazy, Park. That's ancient history."

Sandra flinched. As if he'd struck her.

Ray didn't seem to notice. "Sandra and I are good friends. And now that she's part of the team at the Breeze, she's friends with Roxie, too." He turned to Sandra. "Right, Sandra?"

"Right," she mumbled, her eyes flickering away. She couldn't look straight at Ray anymore. She crossed her arms.

I shook my head. "Sandra only joined the Breeze so she could get closer to you. In fact, everything she's done since you broke up with her has been about getting closer to you. She went to the city and attended bartending school, following in your footsteps. Then moved back to Allington to get closer to you. But recreating your old dynamic— where you needed her to get through your dark days— wasn't so easy. You're happy now, Ray. You've got a thriving business. You've found the love of your life. So Sandra needed to sabotage that happiness."

"She's making all this up," Sandra told Ray.

Ray was silent, a concentrated frown on his face. As if he wasn't just listening—he was thinking things through, piecing the puzzle together.

I said, "Sandra, it's true, isn't it? You decided to tip the balance in your favor. If Ray wasn't unhappy, you'd make him unhappy. First, by hurting his business. You befriended Iggy at Concordia House and offered him money to sabotage the Breeze. But then he demanded more money. Did he threaten to expose you if you didn't pay him more?"

Something flitted across Sandra's face. A hardness. But she said nothing.

I continued. "You couldn't afford to pay him more. But you came up with a neat solution: you'd ask Iggy to do one more job and then kill him, which would damage the Breeze even more than fiddling with temperature gauges on vats."

"Sandra," Ray said, his voice low. He was staring at Sandra with a look of incredulity bordering on horror. "Is this true? Is this how you feel? Is this what you did?"

She looked away. "You're making this up. Where's the proof?"

I said, "The proof is all over town." I raised the dog toy, shaking it in the air as I made my point. I could now see why professors liked to hold pens or pointer sticks. "The posters. Someone was vandalizing them. Defacing them. But each time, a sliver remained. And it was your face, Ray. As if the person didn't want to hurt you."

"See?" Sandra suddenly said, turning to Ray. "I'd never hurt you."

"But Roxie," Ray said. "You tried to run down Roxie?"

"I was trying to make things right between us,"

Sandra said. Her eyes, doe-like, stared at Ray. Pleading. "Get things back to how they should be. But the Breeze recovered. As if Iggy's death had never happened. And the stress of it all, which should've revealed how superficial your relationship is with her—" She seemed to choke on the word. She couldn't even say Roxie's name. "—it only brought the two of you closer together. You risked never waking up to the truth. See? I was only trying to help."

"Help?" Ray pushed off from the bar, sliding off the stool. He backed away from Sandra. "I can't believe I thought you were my friend. You're crazy."

Sandra's face wobbled. Tears sprung to her eyes, and one broke free, trickling down her face. "I'm not crazy, Ray. My sweetheart, please. I know a good thing when I see it. When you find the right one, you hold on and never let go." She dropped her voice to a whisper. The tears were running freely down her cheeks now. "Never let go."

A shiver ran down my spine. It was her mantra, the one she'd scrawled across the pages of her photo album. Ray was right: she was crazy.

Sandra moved around the bar. I glanced at the bar. The knife from the chopping board was gone.

Sandra came around the counter. Her arms hung limp by her sides. In her right, she held the knife.

"I need you," she told Ray. "I need you so bad."

"You've got it all wrong," Ray said. "We were through a long time ago."

"I can't—"

She bit back a sob and raised the knife.

"Freeze," Mom barked, and she grabbed her gun again.

But Sandra didn't listen. She flipped the handle, so the blade turned inward.

Oh, no. She'd said it herself: she'd never hurt Ray. But that didn't mean she wouldn't hurt herself.

I still held the dog toy. It was my only hope of saving her.

Sandra raised the knife, preparing to plunge it into herself.

I pulled back my arm and threw the dog toy at her. It sailed through the air.

Sandra saw it. Her eyes widened, and out of pure reflex, dropped the knife and caught the toy. The knife hit the carpeted floor with a soft thud.

Then there was a happy bark. Wimsey leaped up and bounded toward Sandra. He jumped. Paws out. A bundle of black dots on white ramming into Sandra. She staggered backward.

"No, no, no!"

With Wimsey's paws on her, she tripped and fell. The dog had her pinned to the floor. Alternately licking her face and tugging at the toy. Happy as ever. For a moment, Sandra struggled. Then she went limp and laid back. She closed her eyes, surrendering to Wimsey's playful cuddling. And surrendering to her sobs.

I let out a breath. Mom strode across the room, unsnapping a pair of handcuffs from her belt. I went to Ray and put an arm around him.

"Oh, man," he said.

"Yeah," I said. "Oh, man."

37

"What's this?" Ray cracked open the door to the Breeze. "It's supposed to be locked."

"Are you sure? Maybe Dani got here early."

Ray shook his head. "She told me she'd get to work late today—but that she'd cover in the afternoon so Roxie and I can celebrate my birthday."

"Oh, dang," I said. "I totally forgot. Happy birthday."

Ray waved a hand, dismissing it. "My only concern right now is who got into the Breeze before us."

It was 9 am, a week after the incident with Sandra, and I'd invited myself along to the Breeze. Ray was opening up for the day, checking the brewery, and getting things ready for opening before lunch. Now he looked worried. As if he were thinking the whole sabotage business might be repeating itself.

He pushed open the door and stepped inside. It was dark. The lights were off.

But as soon as we moved inside, I could see shapes in the gloom. So could Ray.

"What the—?" he said.

Then the overhead lights turned on.

He threw a hand up to protect his eyes from the sudden glare.

"Surprise!"

People jumped to their feet. The Breeze was packed, everyone waiting for Ray to arrive. A banner hung above the bar that said, "Happy birthday." The tin ceiling was crammed with helium balloons and confetti covered the tables.

Ray grinned, a dazed look on his face. Roxie came out of the crowd and threw her arms around him. She gave him a long kiss. Then hugged him hard and said, "Happy birthday, my love."

I was grinning like a happy dog.

Scottie came up to me and patted me on the shoulder. "Well done, Park. You didn't mess up."

Mom, Dad, Joy, and Amy converged on Ray, giving him hugs and wishing him a happy birthday. Then the crowd began to sing happy birthday, and Dani, appearing from the back of the restaurant, came carrying a giant cake with candles. The candle flames undulated as she navigated across the floor, holding the platter high. Just as she was about to set it down on a table, her foot caught on a floorboard.

In a flash, Johnny appeared by her side. He put a hand on her elbow to steady her.

"Thanks, Johnny," she said.

She gave him a grateful smile. He nodded and backed away.

She set down the cake on a table.

"You guys..." Ray said, smiling. "I had no idea."

"Total surprise, boss?" Dani asked.

Ray nodded. "Total." He eyed the cake. "Chocolate. My favorite. Who made it?"

I nudged him. "Who do you think, dummy?"

Joy smiled at Ray. "I wasn't going to let your birthday go by without making you a cake."

Scottie held out a bottle of Sugar Glider for Ray.

"It goes well with chocolate," he insisted.

Ray grinned and accepted the offer.

More people gathered around Ray, wishing him a happy birthday.

Aunt Lil gave Ray a big kiss on each cheek and then moved her moonstone wand around him, cleaning his aura.

Johnny, whose gruff attitude had softened around my brother, shook his hand. Balthazar handed Ray a book-shaped package. Half of the town seemed to have turned up for the event. Even Mona was there with her husband.

After she'd greeted Ray, she stepped aside and the two of us talked.

"I hear you're helping Sandra get some help," I said.

She nodded. "She's being held without bail, but your mom and I are finding ways to ensure she has access to a good therapist. The sooner she can get some help, the better."

Mom had kept me updated, of course, and I'd been relieved to hear that Sandra had confessed to her crimes, and that it was likely her sentencing would take into account that she needed counseling. My hope was that she would, over time, let go of her unhealthy obsession, heal, and learn to become the person she was meant to be.

Later, I joined Mom and Dad at the bar and shared my thoughts about Sandra.

"I hope so, too," Mom said.

"And in the meantime," Dad added, "I hope you'll write a Pulitzer Prize-winning story about it all for *The Gazette*."

I put an arm around Dad and then an arm around Mom.

"Oh, I don't need a Pulitzer." I smiled. "I've got everything I need."

THANK YOU for reading this Parker Lee Mystery. Want more? Check out another mystery with Park and her family in:

A Killer View

Want a **free short story**? Sign up for my newsletter to hear when the next book comes out and I'll share the story with you:

https://mpblackbooks.com/newsletter/

If you enjoyed this book, please take a moment to **leave a review online**. It makes it easier for other readers to find the book. Thanks so much!

Turn the page to read an excerpt from *A Killer View*…

38

EXCERPT FROM A KILLER VIEW

"What a perfect day," Mom said.

She and I were finishing lunch on the back porch of the Lakeview Inn, my Aunt Lil's boutique hotel, and it really was a perfect day: the sun sent ripples of silver across Lake Allington. Sailboats drifted past Gull Island. A single-prop airplane soared, albatross-like, high overhead.

We were eating a lunch salad with grilled pear, walnuts, and a thick balsamic. Mom finished the last slice of pear on her plate and put down her fork.

"So, Parker," she said, dabbing her mouth with her napkin, "we've talked about my work—what's going on at *The Gazette*?"

I chewed a slice of pear. A burst of charred sweetness. Then swallowed.

"A guy sighted a northern saw-whet owl in the Allington Woods."

"Wait," Mom said. "A real northern saw-whet owl? That's incredible."

I nodded and smiled. Trying to make my smile look

genuine. Spotting a northern saw-whet owl counted as breaking news, and as a journalist at my dad's newspaper, *The Allington Gazette*, it was my job to cover the story. But once in a while, I couldn't help but miss a big, juicy scandal. Or a shocking crime. The kinds I studied at journalism school. The kinds I covered during my brief stint as a reporter at a major national newspaper in the city—before I got laid off and moved back home.

I'd hoped that lunch with mom would've uncovered something interesting. But these days, crime, like everything else in town, was slow. Allington was peaceful. And that was good, wasn't it? That was what we wanted, right?

"What else?" Mom asked. She brushed a fleck of dust from her uniform. Mom's uniform was, as always, neatly pressed. On her chest, the badge that said "Chief" shone. So did the brass name tag with the "C. Lee" engraved on it. Both spotless. She added, "Are you covering Amy's fundraising events?"

"Of course."

My sister Amy was the pastor at Shepherd's Gate Church, and she was running a series of fundraising events this month. Which, of course, *The Gazette* would cover. In the Lee family, we were all about helping each other.

"But to be honest," I added, "I wish I had something more exciting to report."

"You want exciting?" a voice said.

The door to the inn's lounge opened, and Aunt Lil stepped out onto the back porch. She wore a bohemian kaftan that billowed over her legs. A dozen bangles jangled on her wrists, adding to the rattle of the many necklaces she wore.

"A great flood. The water rising. A desperate struggle against time."

"Is this a mythic story?" Mom asked, sounding skeptical. My mom was the rational one. Aunt Lil was the family mystic. "I mean, are you talking real life here, or are you sharing one of your, um, *insights*?"

"My insights are real life," Aunt Lil said. "Anyway, I'm talking about the basement."

"Ah, I see," Mom said, a little smile quirking her lips.

I frowned. "I don't see."

"I'm guessing a pipe burst," Mom said. "In Lil's basement."

"You're guessing right," Aunt Lil said.

She pulled out a chair and sat down, her kaftan coming to rest along with her clattering jewelry. She told us her story with much hand waving and drama: early Thursday morning she had gone down into the dark basement to get a lightbulb—a lamp in one of the rooms upstairs needed a new one—and she'd stepped right into an inch of water.

"My slippers are ruined. But I'm more worried about the damage to the inn. So I called an emergency plumber, of course. He's down there now."

"That's awful," I said.

I didn't add that it hardly qualified as a good article for *The Gazette*. A burst pipe wasn't breaking news. Even our little local newspaper had its standards.

Aunt Lil must've sensed my reticence, though, because she shrugged and said, "Fine. I can tell you don't want my 'Great Lakeview Flood' story. But that's not all." She leaned forward, a frown gathering on her face. "One of my guests has vanished."

Mom and I looked at each other.

"Vanished?" I said.

"Disappeared." Aunt Lil fluttered her hands in the air. "Poof, gone up in smoke."

"You mean," Mom said, her skeptical look returning, "that you actually saw him vanish in a cloud of smoke?"

Aunt Lil snorted. "Of course I'm not saying that, silly. Don't take everything so literally."

I suppressed a smile. Mom could be too literal. But to be fair, Aunt Lil was also likely to say that someone literally vanished in a cloud of smoke.

"He arrived on Tuesday," Aunt Lil continued. "But I haven't seen him since the day before yesterday."

"Maybe he's gone on a long hike, and he's staying at a shelter in the woods," Mom said.

The Allington Woods, which surrounded Lake Allington and our town, stretched far and wide, reaching up into the mountains in the distance. A great place for hiking. And a pretty good place for getting lost, too.

"He paid cash, one day at a time," Aunt Lil said. "Which means his stuff is sitting in that room free of charge."

The door to the inn's lounge opened and Zadie, the Lakeview's housekeeper, stepped onto the deck. She was carrying a mop and a bucket.

"Zadie," Aunt Lil said. "Any sign of the guest in room 9?"

Zadie shook her head. "The do-not-disturb sign is still on the door."

"Strange..."

"But Lil, one of the guests—Mr. Humphries in room 7—he said a sound woke him Thursday night or early Friday morning. When he looked out the window, he saw someone lurking outside on the dock."

"Lurking?"

"That's what he said. But the person must've seen him. Got right into a boat and rowed away."

"Did he see anything else?"

Zadie shook her head. "He said he was half asleep, and

he didn't have time to put on his glasses. He couldn't even tell whether it was a man or a woman. The person wore a cap that hid their face. And he thought a second person might be rowing the boat. Which, he said, might mean it was just someone out fishing. By the time we were done talking, he'd convinced himself that was the explanation." She frowned. "But why would a fisherman stop at our dock?"

"Yeah, that makes no sense. Zadie, thanks for telling me."

Zadie walked down the wraparound porch and turned the corner.

For a moment, Mom, Aunt Lil, and I sat in silence.

Then I said, "He left his stuff?"

Aunt Lil nodded. "And I've got a bad feeling…"

"He'll turn up," Mom said, sounding unconcerned.

But I wasn't convinced. Mom might be reacting more to Aunt Lil's "bad feeling" than the facts. Yes, my aunt could be a little woo-woo, but she sometimes really did have "insights." Plus, she ran a successful hotel. If she was worried about a guest, shouldn't we take that seriously? And wouldn't a missing guest make a good story for *The Gazette*?

"Maybe we should go take a look room 9," I suggested.

Mom sighed. "Not you, too."

But when I got up, she pushed back her chair, too.

Aunt Lil shot to her feet, her jewelry rattling. She opened the door to the lounge, guiding us through the room full of antique furniture and past the gigantic fireplace. Then into the corridor that led to the reception. Up the old Victorian staircase to the floor above.

"Room 9 is right down this way."

We turned into the right corridor, and Aunt Lil came to a dead stop.

Ahead of us, a person in a black bomber jacket and black baseball cap leaned over the door to a room. Fiddling with the lock.

"That's room 9," Aunt Lil said.

"Hey," Mom cried out. "What do you think you're doing?"

The person glanced back at us. Then turned and bolted, sprinting down the corridor. Sneakers padding the thick carpeting.

I cursed. Then broke into a run.

∼

Want more? Grab *A Killer View* at your favorite online bookstore.

MORE BY M.P. BLACK

A Wonderland Books Cozy Mystery Series

A Bookshop to Die For

A Theater to Die For

A Halloween to Die For

A Christmas to Die For

A Yarn Shop to Die For

A Hair Salon to Die For

An Italian-American Cozy Mystery Series

The Soggy Cannoli Murder

Sambuca, Secrets, and Murder

Tastes Like Murder

Meatballs, Mafia, and Murder

Parker Lee Mystery Series

The Art of Murder

The Deadly Circle

Trouble Brewing

A Killer View

Short stories

The Italian Cream Cake Murder (FREE)

ABOUT THE AUTHOR

M.P. Black writes fun cozies with an emphasis on food, books, and travel—and, of course, a good old murder mystery.

Besides writing and publishing his own books, he helps others fulfill their author dreams too through courses and coaching.

M.P. Black has lived in many places, including Brooklyn, Vienna, and San Jose de Costa Rica. Today, he and his family live in Copenhagen, Denmark, where coziness ("hygge") is a national pastime.

Join M.P. Black's free newsletter to download a free story and get updates on books and special deals:

https://mpblackbooks.com/newsletter/